CHICA *and* NAPOLI

RAMONA A VELAZQUEZ

Archway Publishing books may be ordered through booksellers or by contacting:

Archway Publishing
1663 Liberty Drive
Bloomington, IN 47403
www.archwaypublishing.com
844-669-3957

ISBN: 978-1-6657-5176-6 (sc)
ISBN: 978-1-6657-5177-3 (e)

Library of Congress Control Number: 2023919658

Print information available on the last page.

Archway Publishing rev. date: 10/18/2023

Chapter 1
CAN IT BE?

I AM TRYING TO UNDERSTAND WHAT happened. How did I become Napoli the hated? It was just another day, wasn't it?

As I think back, I remember the day starting like usual. After breakfast, the Papá left for work. With him gone, the Señora started cleaning up the dishes and putting away the food. Nena helped her mother while Moeses started his chores. Panchito, with his Papá's rifle and me close behind, set out to find a long-eared rabbit for the family's supper. It was just another day.

On this trip, we were especially lucky with our hunting. Panchito and I caught two very fat rabbits without even using the rifle. With my incredible speed, I ran them down and snapped their necks before they knew what hit them. Señora Reina, who skinned them and prepared them for the family's dinner, seemed to hug Panchito a little longer than usual.

It seemed like the day flew by. After the table was set for dinner, the family sat and waited for Papá to return home. While the rabbit stew simmered on the stove, Señora Reina reached for her guitar behind the kitchen cabinet and began to play. I remember thinking how her singing filled the casa. As usual, she encouraged her children to sing along. Listening to them had become my favorite part of each day. Comfortably, I watched them through the large window next to my chosen spot on the porch. It was just another day!

Sadly, as had been the custom too often lately, Señor Juan came home reeking of alcohol. I could smell it from where I was resting. As he proceeded to stumble on the pathway to the porch, he yelled, "Reina! I am home. Get the dinner on the table! I need to eat."

I watched as Señora Reina quickly put away her guitar. I noticed how the boys jumped up and walked to the table. Nena moved to her mother's side and began dishing food onto the plates.

My attention turned to my own Mamá, who was quietly drinking water from the box next to the path. I'm not sure whether Señor Juan saw her, but his foot connected with her side. She yelped in pain. A flash of anger shot through my body, and I jumped up from my resting spot on the porch. In a flash, my teeth went after the leg that had caused my mother's pain. I bit into him like I had bitten into the long-eared rabbits I had caught earlier that day and wouldn't let go. He screamed and tried hitting me away. I wanted him to feel the pain I felt he had inflicted on my Mamá.

"You stupid dog! Get off me!"

Panchito ran from inside and pulled me off the Señor while his brother, Moeses, helped his Papá up the steps and to his bed. I watched as Señora Reina ran to the metal tub in the sink, grabbed a towel, and dunked it in water. With the wet towel in hand, she picked up a brown bottle and hurried to her husband. Struggling, Moeses managed to pull off Papá's shoes and pants, exposing the blood on his leg. Panchito, who was holding me in place while I watched the scene unfold, dragged me off to the side of the house. "You're in so much trouble! Stay here! Do you hear me, Napoli? Stay!" When he spoke to me, I detected fear in his voice.

I watched as Panchito ran back into the house. I could hear the Señor yelling over Señora Reina's commands to sit down and hold still. He yelled and groaned. When he was finally quiet, I decided to move back to the open door to see why.

My Mamá was standing there. Her head was turning away from the scene inside and back in my direction. Quickly she walked over to me. I saw the fear in her eyes mixed with tears as she opened her mouth to speak.

"Run, Napoli. Get away from here. You can never come back. If anything happens to you, I will die. Run! Get out of here before he comes for you. He hates you. Leave, leave before he can hurt you. I love you, mi hija."

At this very moment, I understood why I became Napoli the hated. I was hated by a drunken man who called himself a Papá and a husband. I looked over the top of my Mamá's head and saw Señor Juan struggling to stand, using his rifle as a crutch. I wanted to believe my Mamá was exaggerating, but the fear in her eyes and the urgency in her voice told me she was not. I could see Señor Juan trying to raise his rifle, but he was having difficulty. Struggling with the rifle and trying to walk to the doorway seemed to be too difficult a task for this half-naked man.

"Napoli! Napoli! I am going to kill you. Do you hear me, you stupid dog?" It was obvious he wanted me dead.

The children were crying, Señor Juan was screaming my name, my Mamá was pleading with me to run. Oddly, in this moment, I was recalling something she once told me.

"Señor Juan was not always like this. Over the years, he has changed from a loving husband and father to a beer-guzzling shadow of who he was, who now hugs his beers more than his children. Maybe the Señor thinks that alcohol gives him strength to deal with his problems and make his responsibilities less."

I could never imagine him loving me. He had named me Napoli when I was born because he said I was like a cactus, prickly and standing alone. Never fully trusting or needing his attention, I wouldn't go to him like my brothers did. My Mamá and brothers were much closer to him than me. He never liked me. I never liked him. I didn't belong to him like they did.

My name yelled repeatedly snapped me back to this time and place. The Señor was screaming it. I turned my head and saw Nena crying and Moeses with his face in his hands while cowering low against the kitchen wall. They seemed frightened of their father. I watched Señora Reina and Panchito pleading with this crazy hombre to stop. As he ignored their pleas, he continued to slowly limp to the doorway, steadying himself with each step, his rifle at his side.

Still unable to move, I was thinking of what to do. Mamá leaned into me with tears in her eyes. Not wanting to leave her, but knowing I must, I licked her face, turned, and began to run. I was fleeing from the only home I had ever known, from a Mamá who loved me, and from my brothers, who were my closest friends. I ran because I wanted to live, and I knew the Papá wanted me dead. I was out of time. My future was no longer here.

I barked back as Mamá watched me run away. I could hear her respond, "I love you." As I was moving in a stupor-like state from all that had happened, I heard Panchito again pleading with his dad to stop. *My brave Panchito, not afraid to stand up to your father. You are the one human I will miss the most. My Mamá taught me how to run down lizards for food. You taught me how to hunt for rabbits for your stews and our scraps.*

Stopping for a second, smiling from that thought, I turned and saw that I was still not safe. The Señor was leaning against his doorway and trying to raise his rifle. I could still hear Señora Reina pleading with this crazy man. "Think of the kids, Juan. Napoli is a good hunter. Much food comes from her hunting skills. Please, Juan."

My second was up. *Bang!* The rifle behind my Mamá fired a bullet in my direction. It was moving in slow motion. I could see it was about to hit me. The bullet shifted slightly to the right of my head, sounding more like paper ripping. Inches away, it hit. Cactus debris sprayed my face. *That was too close.* I needed to run farther. I needed to be out of his range.

I was running for my life. I now realized I would never be allowed to return. From this point on, I was on my own. I was Napoli, the dog with no home. I stopped abruptly and looked back for the last time at my Mamá watching me. I barked for her ears, "I love you too. Muchas gracias, Mamá, for everything."

Even though I knew Panchito and Moeses would take care of my family, I was feeling an overwhelming sense of loss. Tears were falling from my eyes, and my breath seemed stuck in my throat. "Adios, Mamá."

I turned and started running once more as I heard the ugly hombre's voice yelling, "Napoliiiiiiii!"

Chapter 2

GET ALONG, LITTLE DOGGY

I RAN UNTIL I COULD NO longer hear the voice of the ugly hombre, Señor Juan. My thoughts were with my family. *Will they survive without me? Of course, they will. I give myself too much credit. My brothers are good hunters, just not as good as me. If they work together, they can outshine me. At least if they want to eat, they will.*

I listened to my Mamá. She was the one who felt I needed to leave. She was old, but she was a good hunter. She knew I could not stay there any longer. Señor Juan had never liked me as he did my family, and after what I had done to him, he probably would never forgive me.

I stopped running and tried to catch my breath, turning to look at the casa I had left. I could see the hombre hanging in the doorway. His rifle couldn't shoot this far. He would not chase me. He could barely walk. Again, I thought about my Mamá and my brothers. I knew Panchito and Moeses would look after them. My brothers would take care of Mamá. Moeses and Panchito would take care of Señora Reina and Nena as well.

I felt an overwhelming sense of sadness. My eyes began to water. There was something within me that needed to be released. I stood on all fours, threw my head back, and let out the loudest howl I had ever heard. It was so loud that I saw birds fly away from me and watched as clouds moved in to protect the sun. At this moment, I understood what sadness really means. *I will probably never see my family again. My Mamá is gone. My brothers are gone. Panchito, Moeses, and Nena are no longer part of my life. I will never feel Señora Reina scratch my head again. Everything I love that makes me feel safe is behind me now.*

Coming to my senses, I realized it would be dark soon. Having lived close to the house, I could always hear unfamiliar sounds and urgent cries in the desert from the safety of my porch. My porch was now gone. I needed to walk. I was tired, hungry, and very alone. Even though I had no idea where I was heading, I was comforted by the thought I would not starve. Seeing many lagartos in all directions, my next thought was, *Which one of you lagartos will be my first meal?*

It wasn't long before the biggest lizard I have ever seen was standing in front of me next to a green bush of thorns. It was blinking its eyes and turning its head. I was smiling and thinking, *Are you looking for me, Señor Lagarto? Do you smell me or hear me? You will be quite tender, and I am sure you are no match for my speed.*

Without another wasted moment, I ran. He ran. There was no stopping this race. He was moving so fast on his short little legs. I was surprised that such a fat lizard could still move so gracefully carrying all that weight. I was gaining on him. Just before I was close enough to leap onto his long, wide back, I heard a sound. No, it was a cry. Something was hurting. Where? I stopped. It was Señor Chubby Lizard's lucky day as I watched him run out of my sight.

Standing quietly and listening carefully, I realized the sound was coming from the hill in front of me. No, maybe not. Listening more intently, I turned my attention to the arroyo. Yes. It was coming from that direction. *Keep walking and be careful.* The thought entered my mind, *Could this be a trick—maybe a pack of wild dogs pretending to cry, ready to make me their meal?* I told myself to keep walking slowly. I didn't smell anything strange or confusing, so I kept walking.

The arroyo I was approaching had no water in it. The bottom was thick with lots of sand and slowed me down. After walking a short way, I approached a hill. Cautiously, I climbed the hill following the unfamiliar sound. I was in no hurry. I really wished Panchito were here to lead me.

When I reached the top of the hill, I could hear the cry clearly. As I turned in its direction, I saw some large rocks with a pile of white fur tucked between them. I looked from side to side. I sniffed the air. There was no other movement. No pack of coyotes or wild dogs for me to fear. Instead, the pile of white fur stood, and two dark eyes peeked out. I yelled down, hoping not to scare it. "Are you okay?"

"Who's there? Let me see you. Please come closer." The whimpering voice cracked as it spoke.

It took me a moment to realize that I was talking to another perra just like me. But unlike me, she was very small. She looked slightly older than a puppy, and I could smell her fear. I asked myself, *Why would a perra so small and defenseless be here in this lonely and dangerous place?*

"Hola, Señorita Perra. My name is Napoli, and I would like to be your friend. What is your name, and how did you ever get here?"

Chapter 3
WHERE, OH WHERE, HAS MY POOR DOGGY GONE?

The Señorita had been crying. Her eyes were swollen, and her face was dirty. She had sticks and leaves caught in her fur. She looked at me with her reddish-brown eyes and spoke almost in a whisper. "My name is Chica."

As I took steps closer to Chica, I noticed how her tail began wagging. The closer I got, the more it wagged. Chica lowered her body and seemed to relax. I towered over her as I began to sniff her face. I could see that she instantly trusted me by the way she got up on all fours and sniffed me. It was obvious she needed a friend, a sister, and I was so big and tall next to her. The smell of fear, which I first encountered on a hunting trip with Panchito, had disappeared. I sensed she felt safe with me. "How did you ever get here?"

Chica moved closer to me and sat down on her hind legs. She bowed her head, paused, then looked up into my eyes. I followed suit and sat on my hind legs as well. Sniffing the air, I determined there was no danger. I was ready to listen to what Chica would share with me.

"I was born in a house that was very large. My casa grande had many children and many people to help the children. My mother was beautiful! She had white curly hair like mine, and she was not much bigger than me. She was very loved by the two-legged mother and father."

Chica's eyes grew moist. I nudged her nose with mine. "Go on."

"When all of us were born, my Mamá had made the two-legged parents very happy. We were a litter of three females and two males. All the two-legged children in the house delighted in our births. We had plenty to eat and lots of love."

For a second, I felt just a twinge of jealousy as Chica described her home and her family, especially the part about having plenty to eat. "So, with such a wonderful home and family, how in the world did you get here, Chica?" I asked with a slightly sarcastic tone in my voice.

"Today, my brothers and sisters and I set off on a trip with our two-legged family. We were placed in a big box in the back of the car while our mother sat next to us. We drove for a long time. We passed many fields and open areas with no one living there. We drove through small towns with very few homes. More driving. Finally, we came to a stop. Everyone in the car became very excited. Standing on my hind legs to look out the window, I was surprised to see only water, bushes, and cactuses. No people. No casas. We were in the middle of nowhere."

"You were probably at the beach where my Panchito goes sometimes to play in the water," I told her. "I've heard him tell his Mamá, but I have never seen it. It was too far from our home."

"It was a beach. When we stopped the car, the children yelled, 'We're here! We're at the beach.'"

Chica continued. "Our two-legged family opened the doors of the car and unloaded baskets, chairs, large boxes, and other things onto the beach. After all of that was done, two of the children opened the back of the car and let our mother out. Then they grabbed the box we were in and carried it to their blanket. When they set our box down, someone gently turned the box on its side. We slowly walked out together onto what our mother called *sand*.

"The sand felt so funny. It was hot and stuck to my paws. Our mother watched to see what we would do. I just stepped in it slowly and sniffed it. One of my sisters began to run to the water. My mother ran after her and grabbed her by the back of her neck. We all watched her drag our sister back to where we were standing. Our mother let us know not to walk in that water without her by our side. I understood. We all understood."

As I listened to Chica's story, I could not help but think how lucky she was to have visited the beach. I was concerned that she might go on and on, so I interrupted. "How in the world did you get here, Chica?"

"Well, you see, I have always been very curious. I love seeing and doing new things, much more than my sisters and brothers. My mother would have to scold me a lot for venturing off somewhere. She would always say that I would be the death of her someday. Of course, she would smile, and then laugh."

I could see tears in Chica's eyes. She was missing her Mamá. I was missing mine too. "Chica, I know you are sad and miss your Mamá, but please tell me how you got here."

Chica held back her tears and continued. "As the day went on, the family played in the water, and my mother, sisters, and brothers played in the water too. I really didn't like the feel of the water on my paws, so I looked around to see what animals lived on the beach. While I was sniffing a hole in the sand, I noticed a creature climb out of its hole nearby and walk toward a bush. I had no plans of hurting it. I just wanted to get a better look, so I moved slowly toward it. It must have caught my scent. Before I knew it, I was running after it."

"Oh, Chica! You probably saw a lizard. Lizards are so fast and sneaky. Señor Lizard probably knew you wanted to see him closer and decided to take you for a run. Was he the only one you chased all the way here?" I asked this with a little disbelief. Was Chica that slow that she could not catch Señor Lizard? She really did need me to take care of her.

Chica told me that she had followed the lizard farther and farther up the arroyo and onto a hillside. She admitted she had been so engrossed in catching up to that creature that she had lost track of not only time but also place. She explained that the more she had walked, the more confused she had gotten. Nothing looked familiar.

Chica began to whimper and fell to the ground. Through her tears, she finished by saying, "I have lost my two-legged family and my own family. I didn't even catch up to the lagarto. He left me here while he ran down the back side of the hill. I am dirty. I am hungry. And most of all, I am alone."

I felt so sorry for Chica. I understood what she was feeling. I knew I could turn this hard-luck story around and said, "I can find you something to eat. I can help you with the tangled mess in your fur, but most of all, I want you to know that you are not alone. I am with you, and we will find a new home together. It's all good, Chica. We will be okay."

Chica nodded slowly. I licked her face and told her to wait here until I returned with something delicious. As I walked away, Chica moved back to the spot in front of the two rocks where I first saw her and watched me go.

I sniffed the air. I walked toward a familiar smell, and like a gift from the god in the sky, a fat—no, very fat—lizard scampered from behind a bush and headed toward a hole in the ground. When he reached it, I immediately knew that it was not his hole. The chubby lagarto couldn't squeeze his fat belly in it. That was the opportunity I needed. I ran like the wind was pushing me and jumped on Señor Chubby Lagarto before he could change holes. *Snap*, and he was still. I took him back to Chica.

Chica lay with her face on the ground. I looked at her and she looked up to see me with a long tail dangling from my mouth. I dropped the lizard in front of her. Again, she looked at me and asked, "Do you eat these runners?"

"Of course," I answered. "They are very delicious and very tender. Watch me bite and eat, and then you do the same."

Chica nodded as I bit into Señor Yummy. I was sure Chica had never eaten one of these before. She was probably used to special cuts of meat and chicken, foods that her two-legged family ate. But she was hungry, and before long, I found her nose and mouth buried in the stomach of the lagarto. She chewed and swallowed. By the sounds she was making, I knew that lizard was satisfying her hunger. After I caught a few more lagartos for me, it was time to attend to Chica. She continued to eat as I used my mouth and paws to pull sticks and brush from her fur as best I could.

Once we were finished, she rolled up next to me and licked my paw. She didn't have to say gracias. Her actions spoke louder to me than anything she could have said. I shifted from where I was sitting and moved closer to the giant rock. "Chica, it is late, and we need to sleep. Today has been a very hard day for you and for me. Tomorrow, we will decide what to do next."

I positioned myself so the rock was at my back. Then I lay down. Chica curled up next to me, pressing against my stomach. It was now very dark, and only the twinkling stars overhead and the moon, half its size, could be seen. I rested my head on Chica. I could hear howls in the distance and hooting sounds of an owl close by. There were crackling sounds all around us, but I couldn't imagine what was making them. I could tell by Chica's breathing that she was asleep.

As tired as I was, I couldn't fall asleep. My mind was racing. At one point, I thought I heard Panchito calling me to come home. I knew that was impossible, but at least the thought gave me peace.

As I lay sandwiched between a giant rock and Chica, my mind drifted to my family. The first face to pop into my head was Panchito's. With his wide smile and very white teeth, he was now the man of the house. He had the responsibility to help feed his family. My brothers would have to take my place hunting with him.

I remember the first time I went hunting with Panchito. I didn't know what he expected of me, so I walked closely behind him into the desert. I had never been that far from the house before. As I looked around, I saw the most interesting plants. Bushes and trees were everywhere. Some green with many leaves, and others picked over with only brown twigs hanging from them. There were so many rocks in different formations. But it was the cactuses that really caught my eye. They stood tall with their large, fat arms reaching up.

Panchito must have seen me staring at them. "Napoli, those cactuses with their arms straight up to the sky are over a hundred years old. Their outstretched arms are raised to heaven, reminding us that God is up there and makes all you see possible." I understood. It was God who gave us rocks and provided us cactuses. I liked it when Panchito would teach me something new.

I was still walking closely behind Panchito through the desert when he stopped walking. It was at that moment that l experienced my first real test as a hunter. He slowly raised his finger and pointed to something standing on the dirt road. "Sit, Napoli. Don't move!"

I could see what he was watching and knew what needed to be done. I felt the hair on my back stand up and sensed my nostrils were opening and closing rapidly. I thought that the long-eared, furry animal I was staring at would make a nice dinner for Panchito's family, with leftovers maybe for mine.

We watched as Señor Rabbit sniffed the air. He turned his head and saw us. He began to bolt. Panchito yelled, "Get him, Napoli! Hunt him down like you do with the many lizards you catch."

I took off! Señor Rabbit tried his hardest to shake me, but I was too fast. I followed him between two cactuses that afforded me very little space, and behind some rocks, where he stopped for just a second. That's all it took. I had my mouth over his neck in an instant, picked him up, and shook him. Snap! *He was no match for me. I proudly pranced back to Panchito with Señor Rabbit dangling from my teeth. Panchito was slapping his leg with his straw hat. With my head high, I approached him with my catch.*

Panchito laughed. "Put him down, Napoli. I knew *you would be a great hunter! You will make my mother incredibly happy. Muchas gracias, Napoli. Muchas gracias."*

I felt proud for only a moment before a smaller rabbit darted from the bushes. Its movement surprised Panchito and me, but this rabbit must have sensed danger because he took off so fast it would have been almost impossible to catch him.

Without a word from Panchito, I took off after Señor Straight Ears with the speed of a dog running from death. Up a hill he ran with me in close pursuit. Up he went, then scurried around a rock. I was sure I had him trapped. As I got closer, I felt something was wrong. I stopped for a second. I heard a sound I didn't recognize. Tick, tick, tick. *I smelled something unfamiliar. It was at that moment I saw the biggest snake I had ever seen. The unsuspecting Señor Straight Ears must have run straight for Señor Snake's wide-open mouth. It looked like he had caught Señor Straight Ears's leg, clamping down with such force that he fell to his side. I froze watching Señor Straight Ears's rapid movements change to slow motion.*

I could hear Panchito running up behind me. As he got closer, he saw what I was watching and stood motionless. I could smell fear in Panchito. I had smelled that scent before from my Mamá when Señor Juan would come home drunk from work. When I asked her what that smell was, she told me it was fear.

Panchito said my name in almost a whisper. "Napoli, come with me now. We need to leave here."

I was still watching the ticking snake and wondering if I could pull the rabbit from his grip. Panchito must have known what I was thinking because he grabbed the skin on the back of my neck and began to pull me away. He even turned the bottom of the rifle toward me and hit my backside, whispering to me to go. "Let's get out of here, Napoli!"

Reluctantly, I did as I was told. I could hear Señor Snake shaking his rattling tail at me as if to say, "Come and get it! I have a little surprise for you. Come back, my friend."

I stopped for a second but knew Panchito would be mad if I went back. The smell of his fear began to break apart in the breeze. Panchito then turned to me with a serious look on his face. "Napoli, that snake is extremely dangerous. The desert is full of them. They will usually shake their tail and give you a warning, but not always. Keep your eyes open whenever you hunt and listen for danger. That was your first lesson on being a good hunter. I want to keep you safe and hunting for my family for a very long time."

I understood what Panchito told me. He had a serious tone in his voice. I had stumbled on danger, and fortunately for me, Panchito was there to keep me safe. I vowed to be smarter in the future, and with any new creatures I encountered, I would wait to get the okay from Panchito before I grabbed them.

"Watch and see Mamá squeal with excitement when she sees the rabbit you have caught. I have a feeling this is only the beginning. What a team we make. We're the greatest hunters in all of Baja, Panchito and Napoli."

I found myself smiling. Panchito was so proud of me for catching Señor Rabbit that day. Hearing his laughter in my mind put me at ease. Recalling that memory made me happy. At this moment, with Chica's head buried into my stomach, I felt safe for now.

Chapter 4

LIGHT CAN SHINE FROM THE DARKEST PLACES

SOMETHING JABBED MY BACK LEGS. Suddenly ready to fight, I took a moment to realize what had woken me. Chica had kicked her hind legs into mine. She was running in her dreams. I guessed she was chasing Señor Lagarto to this place. I did not want to wake her, but I knew we needed to get moving. Many dangerous things live here in the desert, and we were now a team in pursuit of a home.

I slowly stood up. With my sudden movement, I jarred Chica awake. She looked startled while jumping to her feet, but then realized who was standing over her. She lowered her head and started to whimper. I imagined yesterday came flooding back to her memory.

"Chica! We don't have time to waste. We need to find a place to call home."

"Oh, Napoli. I miss my family. I miss my Mamá."

"I know, Chica. We have both been through a lot in one day. I miss my Mamá too. Fortunately, we are okay. We are not hurt."

Chica nodded as she raised her head. I think she knew I was

right. Most of all, I sensed she was thankful she was not alone. I was her new sister. We would survive this together.

"Vámanos, Chica! Follow me!"

Chica fell in step with me. I had no idea which direction to walk, but I knew going back was not an option. I chose to not go down the steep hill but instead stay on the flat, high land and try to head away from the sun. I felt that there was a home out there for us. We just needed to find it.

We walked and walked as the sun positioned itself overhead. There were a few cactuses, but no real shade. Occasionally, a brave—or should I say oblivious—lagarto would venture out from his hole or from under a bush, unaware of just how close we were to him. That unknowing creature would be picked off before he could even turn his head. Delicious.

Chica was now used to lizard meat and ate it like it were her last meal. Finding food was not a problem, and we were lucky enough to find small pockets of water here and there. Both of us had the good sense to drink as much as we could at each watering hole. After all, we never knew when we would find water again.

As we walked through the desert, we saw cows, and large black birds who seemed like they were following us on our journey. Fortunately, the snakes I knew that lived in the desert never reared their ugly heads. We really didn't see anything threatening.

Later in the day, we ventured off in search of more water. We found a small watering hole surrounded by cows, and Chica was almost stepped on by one of them. I barked at her just in time to cause her to jump out of the way of two cows needing water. All in all, it was a very good day. We had walked a great distance and had plenty to eat and drink.

That night, we found another large rock to sleep against. Conveniently, we took the same sleeping position we had taken the night before, with Chica tucked against my chest and a large rock at my back.

I was cautious as I rested my head on top of Chica. The desert is a scary place, and most animals that live here die a tragic death. The cactuses live to be old, but not the animals in the desert. I was thankful we were safe for now. I could hear sounds in the distance—so many animals. I let my mind drift to memories of happier times with Panchito's family. I felt myself relax. We were safe for now.

The following morning, we were both abruptly awakened by the sound of howling—loud, obnoxious howling. Then more howls seemed to join the first howl. I could sense something was wrong. I was familiar with those sounds. At my old house, I would hear them in the desert at night. My Mamá said that they were howling sounds of hungry coyotes probably scaring their prey to run from their hiding places. She explained that sometimes they hunted in packs, and nothing was safe from their empty bellies.

The howls seemed to be getting closer. Were we in the path of something they were after, or were we what they were after? Fear set in. "Chica! Get up! We need to run away from those sounds. Stay close to me and don't look back. We must get as far away as possible. Understand?"

Chica nodded her head. Seeing a clearing that was in the opposite direction of the howls and yips, we moved toward it. Chica followed me, keeping up as best as she could, with her short little legs. As much as I wanted to protect her, I wasn't sure if I was up to protecting myself. I had never encountered a coyote before. I didn't know their strength, but I was feeling that their strength was probably in their numbers if nothing else.

"Keep up, Chica! The howls are getting closer and sound like they are separating into different directions. I am guessing they are surrounding us." Fear began to fill my mind, and my long strides took on a sense of urgency.

"Stay up with me, Chica!"

Her little legs were trying their best, but they were no match for mine. Suddenly, I heard a screech and then a growl. I turned around, and saw my sister, my Chica, being dragged by her paw while two other coyotes began moving toward her in anticipation. She was about to become their dinner. *Nooooo!*

I stopped running away and changed directions toward the squealing Chica and the yip-howling threesome. As fast as was possible for me to run, I leaped, full speed, on the culprit who had Chica by her paw. I threw him over onto the ground with Chica still in his grasp. Being larger and thicker than this coyote, I started to bite his head to release her. His mouth opened in pain as he yelped for help. The other two coyotes were in shock over my unwelcome intrusion. For a fleeting second, they were frozen in place. I yelled to Chica, "Run!"

Chica ran to a pile of rocks and scooted in between them with her small body. The coyotes were too large to pursue her into that tiny space. She was unreachable, so they focused their hunger on me. I would provide so much more food than the small one. The threesome reassembled and turned their attention my way. The largest in the pack, who was still smaller than me, shot forward and snapped at my leg, while another snapped at my stomach. Each attempt was met with a growl from me and a snap back. I was holding them off, but I knew the odds of my survival were not good. Three against one are never promising odds. However, I was relieved that Chica was safe for now.

The pack began to step up their game. They had obviously worked together before. They continued to circle and snap at me. I maintained my speed and snapped back. Suddenly, the large one, who I had challenged at the beginning, jumped up on the two rocks where Chica was hiding and growled louder. It must have been a signal, for all at once, the coyotes spread out and tried to get my attention. I could not keep up with all their movements. It was confusing. I was getting careless, and they knew it.

The menacing coyote on the rocks decided it was time to challenge me. He jumped off and landed on my back. Confused, I spun around with him attached to me. The rest of the pack moved closer, and one of them grabbed my leg and bit down. I cried out in pain and fell to the ground. I could smell my own fear as they nipped at me and bit another one of my legs. I couldn't move.

The thought came to me: Was this the way I was going to die? Would I be dinner for a pack of coyotes? I could hear Chica barking and barking from between the rocks. She was scared for me but could not help. I wouldn't give up. I was a hunter and I still had hope.

At that moment, my Mamá's face came into my mind. She was telling me to run. *Run as fast as you can.* I saw Señora Reina squealing with delight as Panchito and I brought her a large rabbit. There was Señor Hissy biting down on the rabbit's foot, and Panchito proudly carrying his Papá's rifle. Why was I seeing scenes from my life? Was I dying?

A sound brought me back to the fight. Out of nowhere came a small explosion. It was a very familiar sound. Was Panchito nearby? The sound made the pack stop and look. The next explosion was closer and pinged off the rocks. This time, the pack backed away from me. Then we all heard the voice of a human.

"Get out of here! Get out or I'll shoot you dead! Yaw! Yaw!"

I could see a man as I lay still on the ground. My body would not let me stand. I tried but could not do it. The man looked old, with lots of gray hair and a dark, wrinkled face. He walked with a limp as though one leg were shorter than the other. His rifle hung down close to his body.

"What have we here? My friend, you were almost a coyote's dinner. Judging from all the blood on the ground, I think I arrived in the nick of time. You're in bad shape, girl, but I know I can help you. Don't move. I need to see how badly you're hurt."

Old man, you saved my life. I tried to wag my tail. Mustering what little strength I had, I called to Chica with two short barks.

Cautiously, she came out from between the rocks, limping and bleeding from her leg wound.

"Why, there are two of you? What are two perras doing out here in the middle of nowhere? Did your owners throw you away in this desert, or did you run away? Well, I know you're not going to answer me. So, I better figure out how I am going to get you home before those hungry coyotes come back with reinforcements."

The old man whistled, and out of the brush came a beautiful horse. I had seen many wild ones before at my old casa, but none were as striking or as gigantic as this one. Maybe he seemed even larger from where I was lying. The old man must have been riding this horse and hidden it from the pack when he moved in to save me.

I saw him pet the nose of this giant and walk to its side. He pulled off a blanket and proceeded to open it on the ground. He was old but very strong. He lifted one side of me and shoved the blanket under, then he lifted my other side and pulled the blanket farther under me. He called for Chica to come to him. I'm sure she could sense he was kind and limped over so he could pet her.

"Well, little perra, you need to climb on the blanket and sit by your friend. I am guessing somehow you got hurt first and your amiga came and fought for you. Coyotes will usually go after rabbits or other small animals before they take on such a large dog as your friend. You lie here and help your companion rest so I can get you two home." Chica did as she was told.

The old man took a rope from his saddle. He threw it onto the ground. Then he walked away from our spot and came back holding a long tree branch. He took out his knife and cut off some of the smaller branches that were attached to the main branch. He slipped the long branch through the top of the blanket.

Next, he tied each end of the branch to each end of his rope. Finally, he centered the rope so that both ends of the rope flanked the horse and wrapped it around the horn of the saddle. The rope was extra-long so that it did not get in the way of the horse's back legs. I saw a smaller rope on the other side of the saddle and wondered why he had two. I could not help but think he had dragged other animals home like this before. He seemed to know what he was doing.

"Okay, Cisco! Let's go home," the old man told the horse. "We do not have any food to show for our day, but we do have some new mouths to feed. Vamos, Cisco!"

The old man walked in front of the horse, leading it by the reins. I felt every bump and lump through the blanket as we moved along on the dirt road. Chica stayed so close to me that her weight pressed firmly against me. I felt weak, and my whole body was in pain, but I was so thankful that the old man had come when he did. I recalled him saying that he now had *new mouths to feed*. That could only mean that Chica and I had finally found a new home. He seemed like a kind man, and I knew that when I was strong again, he would see what a great hunter he had saved. But for now, I could only close my eyes and hope that this pain would go away soon. I felt hopeful. Maybe our search was over.

Chapter 5

HOME IS WHERE THE HEART IS

THE OLD MAN WALKED AND walked for what seemed like forever. I had never known physical pain like this before. Chica and I had been saved from a pack of hungry coyotes by this kind old man who dragged us behind his horse as he led it by the reins. His actions told me he cared about Chica and me; this human was guiding his horse on foot. For a moment, my body seemed to rise above the pain. I felt such happiness. How could we be so lucky?

Just when I was about to close my eyes again, I heard Cisco neigh and watched him throw his head back, trying to pull the reins from the old man. "Cisco, you're home, but we still have some passengers to take care of here. Head toward the stable. We will drag the blanket into your area of the barn. Slowly, Cisco, you are doing a great job!"

When we finally reached the barn, the old man spoke once more. "Stop, Cisco! Give me space to open the doors."

The horse stopped in front of two giant white doors. The old hombre unlatched both, pulling them as wide as they would go. Grabbing Cisco's reins, he slowly led the horse inside. I noticed how the ground felt so smooth under the blanket that was dragging us.

I watched as the old man untied the rope from his saddle and threw it behind Cisco. Then he reached under Cisco's large belly and undid a strap. He grabbed the saddle and pulled it off, mounting it on a wooden bench. After removing a small blanket from Cisco's back, he slapped the horse, and it trotted to a stall. "That must be his space," I whispered to Chica.

The old man proceeded to untie the blanket we lay on from the branch that had supported the blanket. After he rolled up the rope, he bent over and spoke to Chica and me. "Do not worry, perras. Have faith. Things have a way of working themselves out. Rest here. I'll be right back."

He walked through the doors, latching them behind him as he left. I wasn't afraid. I had no way of leaving even if I had wanted to run. I could feel Chica shaking while she lay against me.

"Chica, don't be afraid. That hombre is a kind hombre. His actions speak of a kind heart. He brought us here. He will take care of us. Somehow, with all we've been through, we will be rewarded with a good home. You'll see."

Right after I said those words, the old man unlatched the doors and walked through one of them. He was carrying a basket in one arm and holding a pail in the other. He sat down beside us on the ground. The pail contained water. He took two bowls from the basket and dipped each into the water. He placed one by my mouth and one by Chica's. Chica sat up and slurped the water. I could only raise my head slightly. The old man tried to lift me over the bowl, but my face fell into it, causing the water to spill onto the blanket. The old man dipped the bowl in the pail, filling it once again, and held it under the side of my mouth. While I was on my side, my tongue reached for the water. It was a slow process, but eventually, I was able to drink.

Next, the old man put a large rag in the pail of water. He wrung it slightly and proceeded to wipe my wounds gently. The water felt good on my fur. He rinsed his rag and did it again. I had so many wounds I wasn't sure if he would ever stop, but finally, he did. Then he did the same for Chica's wounds. I could no longer see blood on myself or on Chica. The lack of blood exposed deep cuts all over my body. Fortunately, Chica's wound was not as deep and only on her paw.

"Perra Grande," the old man said, "I will have to tape up the wounds on your legs, and hopefully, you will let me do that on your side as well. I would try to sew you closed if I had someone else here to hold you down. If God is willing, he will help me fix you as good as new." He pointed to the sky when he said *God*. For a second, I was reminded of the cactuses Panchito had told me about.

"Perra Pequeña, I will clean the wound on your paw first. You are very lucky, only one deep wound. I think your amiga saved you from being coyote dinner. You are the perfect size to eat." Chica put her face down on the ground. She didn't want to hear any more. It scared her that she had been so close to dying. She leaned over and licked my face.

"Si, Perra Pequeña. You are thanking the one who you owe your life to. She saved you and I saved her. Now let's get the both of you mended."

The old man pulled out a small can and unscrewed the lid. With his finger, he scooped up a small portion of the cream in the can and pressed it into Chica's wound. She whimpered while he was doing this.

Next, he scooped up a larger portion from the can and looked at me. "Perra Grande, this will hurt, but it will help you heal. Trust me. I want you to get well, and this will make that happen. Now relax. I will be quick."

I lay there while he gently smeared the cream in my deepest wound. I felt a sharp pain. Instinctively, I jerked my head, exposing my canines. He calmed me down with his gentle touch and his calm voice.

"I know this stings, but it will make you well again. I promise. Hold still."

I sat still, knowing this old man was telling the truth. He was easy to trust, and I wanted to be well. He continued placing cream on my remaining injuries. I believed that the burning pain I was feeling was killing all the coyote spit that was there. *Keep it burning, old man. I want to be well again.*

After he was done attending to all my injuries, he stood up and collected the things he had brought. Slowly, he walked out the open door and closed it behind him. Chica curled up next to me. We both had a desire to sleep, and so we did.

Chica and I awoke when we heard the door open again. It was much later in the afternoon. I could not believe we had slept so long. The old man walked in with a rag and the can of cream from before. No pail of water this time. I guessed it was because we were no longer bleeding, and we still had water in our bowls.

"Perra Grande and Perra Pequeña, how are you feeling? I see you must be doing better because your wagging tails give you away. I need to put more of this medicine on you, por favor."

This time, when the old man put cream on my wounds, it did not hurt quite as much as before. He smiled with each swipe. I could tell by the way Chica reacted that it did not hurt her either. She started to lick her wound.

The old man told her, "Perra Pequeña, no licking. It needs to heal first." And he reached for her mouth and pushed it away. Chica understood and lay back down.

The old man stood up and left again through the open door. It remained open. This time, he came back with water and topped off the bowls he had left us. He set one under my mouth and one next to Chica. She could stand up and slurp her water. I could raise my head higher than earlier that day and slurped mine as well.

"Let's see if you can eat some food." The old man walked away and returned with pieces of something. He proceeded to tear them into small bits.

"Okay, perras. We have chicken on the menu today," he said. "You like chicken?"

I stared at him, wondering what he meant. I remembered those feathery birds that ran around the yard at Panchito's house, which I left alone. I knew they left eggs for Nena to collect, but I had no idea they were food.

The old man threw his head back and laughed. "I see you are not so sure. This chicken will have to do until I can have my beautiful daughter, Maria, bring a bag of dog food from town. I called her this morning, and she will be out soon with my groceries and your food. But for now, you need to eat this."

I had only ever eaten fish, rabbit, and lizards before. Panchito didn't like fish, but his Mamá made him eat it. He would put it under his leg at the table, and when he was excused, he would bring it out to my family and me. I liked the flavor and never understood why Panchito didn't. Chicken would be something new.

"Okay, Perra Grande. Don't bite the hand that's feeding you." The old man laughed as he slowly put pieces of chicken in my mouth. It was nice to have someone feed me. I knew it would not be long before I was my old self. I just needed to be patient.

The old man laid the pieces for Chica on the blanket. Chica stood up and began eating the food that was placed in front of her. I wished I was in as good of shape as Chica. *Patience.* The old man walked out of the door and closed it behind him.

It wasn't much later when a honking car pulled up to the barn. We could hear the old man talking and a young, higher-pitched voice answer back. I remembered the old man saying that his daughter would be coming by. I figured it must be her.

The barn door opened, and in walked the old man and a much prettier version of himself. The young woman bore a striking resemblance to the old man. She was shaking her head from side to side and speaking to her father loudly.

"Papá! Where did you find these stray dogs? The big one looks like she is very lucky to be alive. When did you decide to be a nurse instead of a rancher? Hmmm? And do not smile at me like that. Another mouth to feed? Two mouths to feed! You have a kind heart, Papá, but dogs cost money, and money is in short supply."

The old man grinned. "Ah, Maria, my beautiful and practical daughter. I believe these dogs will bring me luck. After all, they were on death's doorstep when I found them. I think the big dog is special."

"What do you mean, Papá?"

"Coyotes usually don't attack big dogs, so I am sure they were after the little dog and the big dog risked her own life to save her."

Maria smiled. "You are impossible! Your heart is as big as this barn, and I know for sure that is the main reason why Mamá loved you, and why I love you."

"Besides, Maria," the old man responded, "the big dog is a female, and females are good hunters. I think she will eventually help me on the ranch. You'll see."

"Okay, Papá! You win as always. Next Wednesday, when I come to bring groceries, I will remember to bring another bag of dog food too. You're probably right. Maybe they'll be good hunters and, I hope, good companions for you."

"That's the spirit! And that's why you are my favorite daughter," the old man said with an even larger smile.

"Funny Papá. I am your only daughter." At that, the old man threw his head back and laughed.

"By the way," Maria added, "I heard from José Luis, your favorite and only son." The old man smiled this time. "He says he has been too busy selling his art in the city to travel right now. There seems to be an interest in his work. He told me to tell you he is sorry, but at this time, he cannot come and see you. Mexico City loves him, and he wants to stay as long as they'll buy his paintings. He hoped you'd understand."

I watched the old man's expression. It went from a big smile to a small one. He looked down at the dirt. Maria reached out to him and grabbed his arm. "Don't worry, Papá. He will come eventually. At least you have the most beautiful member of the family here to take care of you."

"You are so right! You are my gift from God. Every night, I pray to God and to your beautiful mother, thanking them both for giving me you," the old man replied.

"Well, there you go. Come on and help me unload the groceries, Papá. I must pick up your grandchildren in an hour from school, so I will be here a shorter time today."

"No problema, mi hija. I am always thankful for any time you can spare for me. As for José, I tell myself to have faith. I believe things always have a way of working out. José will come someday, God willing. Let's get those groceries."

As I watched the old man and Maria walk out of the barn, I was touched by how much love they had for each other. I felt a small tear form in my eye as I was thinking of my own Mamá. I had a feeling that Chica was doing the same.

"Okay, Chica," I began, "we have a home. We have a family. Most of all, we have each other. We both miss our Mamás, but we are still alive, and maybe someday, we will see them again. For now, mi amiga, we will make the best of our new family. I have a feeling the old man needs us. We will show him that his bravery and kindness to us was worth it."

Chica barked once and lay back down. It was time for another siesta. We both needed to sleep, which I figured was probably helping us heal. Chica curled up against me as she had been doing, and I rested my head on her. We were home and we were safe—such a nice thought as we drifted off.

Chapter 6
HOME, HOME ON THE RANGE

Two weeks had passed, and I was basically feeling like myself again. My body was a little stiff, but I knew I was healed. Chica had healed faster and had been in the yard every day, chasing lizards and barking at the chickens. She loved the old man, and I could tell he loved her too. Who wouldn't? She was tiny with lots of white curly hair, and she loved to dance in a circle on her hind legs. When she barked, it seemed like she was talking to the old man, and he would answer her back with his words.

I was big and brown, and not as cute as Chica. But that was okay. I knew I was a hunter that possessed great speed. I also knew that most animals in the desert were not interested in having me for their dinner. Chica, on the other hand, was just the right size for a mountain lion's or coyote's meal.

One morning, the old man said to us, "Okay, my perras. You are ready to hunt with me. I am not so sure about you, Perra Pequeña. You will need to stay close. I have a feeling more animals will be interested in hunting you. Perra Grande, you will be my right arm. You will run into the brush and scare the animals out of hiding.

After I shoot the rabbits and birds that flee, you will fetch them and bring them to me. Let's see if you're a good hunting dog."

Panchito carrying his father's rifle popped into my mind. Of all things to think about, I could hear Señora Reina yelling at him not to shoot off his foot. I had hunted with a young boy, and now I would be hunting with an old man. I wondered what the difference would be as I waited for us to leave.

The old man whistled for Cisco, who trotted out. The old man grabbed his small blanket and put it on Cisco's back. Then he tossed his saddle on top of the blanket and pulled the strap under Cisco's fat belly. Next, he grabbed the large blanket that Chica and I had been sleeping on every night, shook it, folded it tightly, and placed it in the basket on the side of his saddle. His two ropes, rolled in circles, slipped nicely into his other basket, hanging from the other side of the saddle. Finally, he attached a bag to his saddle horn, which fell to the front side of the saddle.

The old man briefly walked away and returned with his rifle. It was the same one that had saved Chica and me from those hungry coyotes. "I have my rifle, and everything else is ready to go. Okay, perras, onward to catch me some dinner. Stay close. There are snakes, cactuses, and maybe a coyote or two along our path. Follow close behind me."

The old man lightly kicked Cisco's side, and off we went. My body felt stiff as I ran close behind the giant horse. Chica, with her short little legs, was going to be doing a lot more work than me in keeping up. I had hoped the old man would know to stop occasionally so Chica could catch up to us, but he stared straight ahead, unaware of what was happening behind him.

A horse goes so much faster and farther than a thirteen-year-old boy hunting on foot. I knew it would take all of my strength to keep up with Cisco and the old man, so I pushed myself. I was out of shape, but I wanted to impress him, and knew I would eventually get my chance.

I barked back to Chica, "Come on, Chica. Run faster! Get those short legs working. I will wait for you to catch up, but I know Cisco will not be waiting. So run, Chica, run."

It did not take long for me to feel like my old self. That first run got everything working again. Chica was truly winded, but I never let her get too far behind. I would stop where I could see her and still see the old man. Once she caught up to me, off I would run again. After doing this for a while, Cisco finally stopped. I barked back at Chica that we were stopping. She moved faster to where I was, and we both joined the old man as he tied Cisco to a tree.

"Okay, perras, this is where we move on foot to find our food. We don't want our prey to know we're looking for them. Silencio!" he whispered with his finger to his mouth.

As the old man led the way, we followed quietly. Suddenly, the old man stopped and began to raise his rifle. I sniffed the air and sensed the familiar smell of a rabbit close by. I slowly moved forward and could see him nibbling on a bush completely unaware of what stood only yards from him.

Why waste a bullet? The old man did not know he was with the fastest rabbit hunter in all the area. Just as he started to take aim, I jumped out from behind him and raced toward the very unsuspecting, chubby rabbit that was almost in his rifle's view.

"Ah, Perra Grande, you'll scare him off. What's the matter with you?" the old man yelled in my direction.

I could hear his frustration, but he didn't know I wasn't done yet. I kept running even though I could hear him calling me back. I could see Señor Chubby Rabbit as he turned and ran to the bushes. *You are not getting away from me.* I picked up speed. I felt like I could fly. As I got closer, I saw that Señor Chubby was not holding his own. He was not as fast as his skinnier cousins. I was almost on top of him when I reached down and clamped onto his neck. I shook him as hard as I could and heard the familiar cracking sound. Señor

Chubby Rabbit was dead. I proudly marched back with the catch hanging from my teeth.

The old man spotted me and, like my friend Panchito, proceeded to slap his leg with his hat. "Perra Grande! You caught the biggest catch of the day, and I didn't have to fire my rifle. You have the speed of a wildcat. You are the hunter I have always dreamed of owning. Oh, gracias Dios for bringing these perras to me. I am sure my wife had something to do with this too. My beautiful wife looks out for me in heaven. Muchas gracias, my love!" the old man yelled out as he was looking to the sky.

My actions had made him happy. He was even dancing a little. I wanted to please him, and I had succeeded. Chica, not to be outperformed, jumped up on the old man's leg holding a small fat lizard in her mouth. The old man took it from her and thanked her as he put the rabbit in the sack with the lizard on top. The old man was through for the day. He had something to show for his trouble. He needed to take our meaty catch home, skin it, and cook it. He was very appreciative of my efforts.

That night, he gave Chica and me some cooked rabbit and the lightly cooked lizard, along with our dry dog food. We were feeling full and very happy. This was now our home, and today, we had earned our keep.

After dinner, the old man sat on the porch with his guitar in his arms and started to sing. He sang to the night sky. He sang and sang. Chica began to yip to his songs. The old man laughed and told Chica she was a good singer. I just lay on the porch and listened. I was sure the old man was singing to his wife, for whenever he mentioned her, he looked to the sky.

The old man smiled, bowed his head, and took off his hat each time he finished a song. Maybe he was waiting for the applause he deserved. Maybe that was the way he honored his wife. Our tails wagged in appreciation after each hat tipping. Chica would even bark.

Finally, after many songs, the old man rose to walk inside. His leaving was usually our signal to go back into the barn and sleep. But before he went in, he spoke to us. "Perra Grande and Perra Pequeña, you have proven that you are great hunters. I need to honor you and, most of all, take care of you. God in heaven gave you to me, so I will return the favor and protect you. From now on, both of you will sleep in my casa. No more barn for you. The barn is for my beautiful Cisco. You are now my family, and a family takes care of each other. I don't think we'll mention the sleeping arrangement to Maria quite yet. You know how she lectures me. But I will tell her what great hunters you are. Praise be to God!"

From that day forth, Chica and I hunted and played all day with the old man. At night, we slept in the house by his fireplace. Whenever Maria came, the old man showed her how many rabbit skins he had collected that week. He would say that he did not waste a bullet. Instead, I was his bullet. He would brag that I was the best hunter in all of Mexico. Of course, he would mention Chica too! He would say she was the second-best hunter in Mexico. Chica would bark her appreciation for the compliment. There was always happiness in the old man's house. His god had been good to all of us.

After much time had passed, Chica and I found that Maria began to accept us as family. She knew we were good for her father. She could see his joy each time she visited. Occasionally, she would bring some scraps of food for us, and tell her Papá, "I have lots of leftovers. Eventually, I would have thrown them out, anyway."

Chica would perform for the food by standing on her hind legs and dancing in a circle, which delighted Maria. I would sit quietly until she called for me, showing her I was not only a great hunter but also a very obedient dog. It took many months, but we finally won Maria's heart. To have two humans who love you and take care of you, what could be better? I wished my Mamá could have had this experience instead of the one I left her in, back in my old casa.

I loved the days when Maria would bring her son, Felix, and her daughter, Anna, to see their grandpa. On those days, the old man would be so happy. He would always have candy waiting for them. After Maria would drive up, Felix and Anna would jump out of their car and run into the old man's arms. After lots of hugs, he would pull out treats from his pockets. There was so much love.

Maria would head to the kitchen to drop off groceries. "I'll put away these groceries while you relax, Papá. Then I'll make all of us some lunch."

I could see she was happy her Papá loved her children. The old man would play with them until he got tired. Once he sat down and pulled out his handkerchief to wipe his face, it was our cue to move in and take over for him.

Felix was older and rougher than his sister. "Okay, Perra Grande, see if you can get this stick and bring it back to me." He loved throwing sticks for me to retrieve, along with balls and the occasional toy. He would smile and thank me when I would bring them back and place them at his feet. I loved entertaining Felix.

Chica, on the other hand, played only with Anna. Chica did not run for sticks or balls. Instead, she would dance with Anna and let her clip bows in her fur. Chica loved the attention, and the little girl felt that Chica was her dog. When she dressed Chica in paper clothes with bows to match, she would have Chica model the latest outfits. "Mamá, come in here. I want you to see the clothes I made for Perra Pequeña. Wait until you see how beautiful she looks."

Maria would always applaud Anna's creations. Even the old man would throw out a comment or two assuring Anna she would be a famous dress designer someday.

The children brought so much joy. It was hard for them to leave, and it was hard for us to watch them go. The home of the old man was full of love. Chica and I were so lucky. I could never forget what it was like to be afraid, as I had been in the home of the mean Papá. Our old man was nothing like the ugly hombre I had left behind. Maria and her kids were the extra blessings for all of us to enjoy.

Late at night, I would watch the old man kneel next to his bed, fold his hands, and speak to the sky. He would thank God for all his good fortune, for Chica and me, for Maria and her children, and for his son, José Luis, who Chica and I did not know. "God, help José Luis find his way home." I could tell the old man missed his son terribly. "Also, God, would you mind giving my wife a big hug and kiss from me? Gracias. Amen."

Then he would climb into bed. Chica and I would take our places in the main room, with Chica curled up beside me and my head resting on her. Each day was wonderful! I was so happy to be Napoli, Perra Grande and hunter magnificent. Each night as I closed my eyes, I would think about how everything was perfect.

Chapter 7
ALL GOOD THINGS MUST COME TO AN END

Chica and I had a wonderful life with the old man. Every day was filled with laughter and love. We had plenty to eat and not a care in the world. The only thing expected of me was to hunt with the old man. That was not a job but something I loved doing, especially if it made him happy. I looked forward to waking up every day, and because of the old man, every day was joyful.

One morning, the old man greeted Chica and me by saying, "Okay, my beautiful perras. It is time to rise and shine. I have made too many scrambled eggs for my plate, which leaves some for you. But if you don't pop up soon, I'll be obligated to throw them to the chickens."

The old man smiled, knowing we were not going to let that happen if we could help it. Up Chica and I jumped, and off we went to where our bowls stood. We watched the old man lean over and scrape the eggs almost equally into our bowls. Of course, I was bigger and deservedly received more. Chica and I waited until the old man gave us his okay before we ate our special treat. The old man turned and dropped his dish in the sink before sitting down at the table.

I had been noticing lately that he seemed to be moving slower. We did not hunt as much, and he didn't sing as much as he used to. Something was different in him. I could feel that things were changing. He was very tired and would even let his dishes pile up in the sink before he washed them.

"Okay, my faithful friends. Maria is coming this morning to bring us our supplies for the week. She will be traveling to the United States of America to visit with José, who will be showing his art in San Diego. She wants to leave right after she sees us. She will be flying into Tijuana and crossing the border to San Diego. Felix and Anna will remain in town with their Papá at his house.

"Maria says that she will be staying with her cousin David, who lives in Chula Vista. She hasn't seen her cousin in two years, so this trip will also give her a chance to catch up with him. He will drive her to see José's art show, which is being held at a very fancy place. Maria told me that people say José is so good at what he does that they have special showings of his paintings. That makes me proud. Maybe he will fly down here someday so you can meet him."

The old man smiled and continued. "People used to say he looked and acted like me. But I see my beautiful wife in his eyes, and he inherited his wonderful artistic gift from her as well. She was the artist. She did all the paintings on my walls. She had so many talents. Someday soon, I will join her in heaven, and we can talk and hold each other again." His face looked peaceful. "Enough jabbering! I need to get ready for Maria's short visit. She will run in and run out." He slowly rose from his chair.

"Maria said she will only be in San Diego for three days. She promised she'll bring the kids with her on her return and spend more time with stories of her trip." The old man drifted off into his thoughts for a moment. I wondered what he was thinking about.

Then Chica barked and the old man snapped out of it. "You're right, Perra Pequeña, no time to waste." He got up from the table and proceeded to get ready.

A few minutes later, a honking car pulled up in front of the house. It was Maria, and we all went outside to greet her. She hugged her Papá and kissed him on the cheek. She hurriedly pet Chica's head and then mine. I could tell she was not staying long.

"Papá, I am running late. I will not be able to help you put the groceries away. I'm sorry. The kids are finishing their packing and waiting for me to take them to their Papá's casa before I drive to the airport. I am so excited, but I am feeling overwhelmed. You should be fine until I return. I cannot believe I get to see José's paintings in San Diego. Wouldn't Mamá be proud of her son? If there's time, I will see you midweek with the kids and lots of photos and stories to tell. In case of an emergency—"

The old man cut her off. "Stop worrying about me. I am thankful each time you bring me anything. Of course, I can put it all away without you. I have Perra Grande and Perra Pequeña to help me. Just leave the bags on the porch and I'll take them in. You need to hurry. Give my love to José. Have a wonderful time, and please take lots of pictures. I can't be there, but I want José to know I am interested in his art. Tell him he takes after his Mamá."

"I will, Papá. I love you with all my heart. You two take care of Papá, okay?" We both barked on cue, which caused the humans to laugh.

Maria set the bags on the porch, kissed her Papá, and jumped back into the car. She drove away honking and waving. All three of us stood there watching until we could no longer see her car. It was then that the old man turned to us.

"Well, these groceries are not putting themselves away. This is the only time I wished you two had arms so that you could help me."

Chica and I watched the old man open the screen door, placing a block of wood at the base to hold it open. There were three bags sitting on the porch. The old man moved slowly as he bent over and began lifting the first bag into his arms and walking it into the kitchen.

It was an unusually hot day, and with each bag he lifted, the old man would let out a sigh or a small grunt. I watched him and worried that he seemed almost too weak to carry them. Something was not right. He usually moved faster. For the first time in my life, I wished I had arms to help him. He needed help. I was thinking, *If only Maria had helped him.* Something was not right.

The old man was carrying the last bag inside when I heard a crash. Chica and I ran in from the porch and saw him on the floor with the groceries scattered around him. He was groaning and holding his arm. I felt completely helpless, watching him twisting and moaning.

"Oh, perras, something is very wrong. My arm is so painful. I feel weak. Look at this mess. Maria will be very upset."

I rushed to the old man and nudged him with my head to get up. Then I tried licking his face. He didn't try to push me away.

"Oh, the pain. I can't move. I feel so tired. I just need to close my eyes for a second and rest. That's what I need. I need to rest." Those were the last words he said before he fell asleep.

Chica and I started barking. I am not sure why we chose to do that, but barking is one of the things we do when we are afraid.

"Napoli, why is the old man sleeping on the floor with all those groceries around him?" Chica asked me. "He's never done that before."

"I know, Chica." Cautiously, I walked to the old man, standing above him. "Oh please, old man, please get up. Please wake up. We need you."

Instinctively, Chica started licking the old man's face. I joined in. We kept licking his face, his eyes, and his ears. I tried to stick my head under his hand and then under his arm. He wasn't responding. He wasn't petting my head. He wasn't pushing me away. Was he sleeping that deeply?

Maybe I was scared for nothing. He had taken siestas before and would wake up and start his dinner. But he took siestas in his bed, not on the floor, and not with groceries all around him. *Please, old man. This does not feel right. We need you to wake up. Please wake up.*

Chica and I just looked at each other. "Maybe the old man is taking a siesta," I said.

"But, Napoli, he has never taken one this early."

"I know, Chica. All we can do now is wait and see. If it is a siesta, he will wake in time for dinner. He has never missed dinner."

The day seemed longer than usual. At one point, I got up and pushed away the wood block holding the door open. I knew the old man would never leave his door open that long. He would always tell Felix and Anna to close the screen door, so bugs didn't get in the house.

The sun was setting over the mountains. It was the old man's dinner hour. Chica and I went to our water bowls. There was very little there. We drank what was left. Our food bowls were empty. We both walked back to the old man. He was not moving. He felt cold when we tried licking his face.

The old man was not moving. He was not breathing. We needed Maria. She would make it right, but I knew we were not going to see her for a while. I had this sad feeling that the old man would never wake again.

We needed to go find Maria. We had been to her casa in town a few times. We could wait for her there. We were not any good here. *She is on a trip but will be back soon with groceries.* I found it difficult to think clearly. The old man was not waking up. Maria was gone. It was dark outside, and there was no light in the house.

"Oh, Chica, I don't know what to do. Is the old man sleeping? Or is he never going to wake again? Maria will know what should happen. Let's try to sleep and figure out what to do in the morning. Maybe the old man will wake up." I took my place near the old man's legs. Chica curled up next to my stomach, and I rested my head on her. I could feel her shaking. I knew she was scared. I was scared too.

"It will be okay. Go to sleep now. We will figure it all out tomorrow. Close your eyes, Chica. It will be all right."

Chapter 8
WHY?

CHICA WAS THE FIRST TO awaken. I could feel her movement, and for just a second, I woke up feeling happy. Then I looked around the room. The old man was on the floor, and the groceries were scattered everywhere. I felt a heavy weight on my head. I had to admit to myself that the old man was dead. He had come into our lives when we were almost dead and saved us. He had shared his home, his love, food, and his family. He had provided the best life for Chica and me.

"Napoli, is the old man sleeping?" Chica asked me.

"No, Chica. I think he's dead."

There was a pause. I could see she was thinking about what I had said. "I'm hungry. When's he going to feed us?"

"Chica, he's dead."

She stared blankly. "So, later?"

I shook my head. "It doesn't work like that. The old man will never wake up again. We need to think about what we are going to do." Chica's eyes began to water.

"I know, Chica. I feel sad too. The old man was very good to us. He gave us a home and a family. We need to find Maria and let her

know. We also need to find food and water. There is no old man to take care of us anymore."

Chica began to make sounds I had never heard from her before. Her cries were long and painful. I found myself joining in until I broke into a howl. Chica and I howled and howled and howled. The best thing in my life was gone, and now we needed to rely on ourselves once again.

It was not long after we stopped howling that we both realized we were hungry. I knew we would not starve. There were always lizards for us to eat. But at that moment, I became aware of some smells in the room.

"Chica, let's see what's in the bags. We can fill our bellies and then think about finding Maria." Chica nodded.

The bag that had fallen on the floor with the old man had only contained vegetables. Most of the items had remained in the bag except for the potatoes, which had rolled to various spots on the floor. Nothing in that bag appealed to Chica or me.

Unfortunately, I knew that it would fall on me to get the remaining food in the bags on the counter. The bags were too high for Chica to reach. I stood on my hind legs and grabbed a bag with my teeth. I pulled and pulled.

Finally, with one last tug, the first of the remaining two bags fell off the counter. A white liquid Maria called *milk* poured out of a large container. We had never tasted it before, but it was the old man's favorite. Maria bought it just for him. We licked it up. It was so good. We pushed the container around so that the milk continued to pour out of it.

After we had our fill, I jumped up one more time and pulled the remaining bag off the side of the counter. It fell to the ground, and all sorts of things spilled out. I recognized one of the packages. It had meat in it. The old man would cook it on the stove, and it would smell so delicious.

The meat was wrapped in paper, so I bit into it and shook it around. Some meat dropped from the paper, so I shook it more. By then, most of the meat was spread out on the floor. We both attacked it. It had a warm taste. The old man had given us scraps from his plate before that tasted a little different. No matter, it was so much better than the dry food we usually ate. I liked it even more than rabbit meat. We ate as much as we could, and there was still meat left over.

It was time for our morning nap. Our stomachs were full, and we still didn't have a plan. I knew we would have to go for help, but for now, we would sleep.

As I tried to nap, something didn't feel right in my stomach. Chica was acting like she was not feeling well either. She and I both stood up at the same time and ran in the direction of our water bowls. Before we reached the bowls, we started to spit up everything we had eaten. It hurt when it came out. We both left piles of food from our stomachs on the floor. My head hurt. My stomach hurt. Chica and I looked at each other, confused.

"Chica, there was something wrong with the milk and the meat. Don't eat it again. Something in it made us sick. We need our strength. That food was unfamiliar to us. We need water."

I looked around the room. The old man kept a giant bottle of water on a stand in the corner. I knew that if we tipped it over, the water would spill out. I tried to hit the stand with my head. It hardly budged. Then I tried hitting it with my head higher on the stand. That didn't work either. So, I stood on my hind legs and pushed with my paws. The water bottle slid on the stand. I did it again and again until I pushed the bottle against the sink. I looked around and saw a chair. I slid the chair with my nose to the bottle. This time, I climbed up on the sink and leaped on the water bottle. That did it! The stand, the water bottle, and I toppled over. Water went everywhere. Water even puddled around the old man and the groceries.

"Chica! Drink, Chica! Fill your belly."

Chica and I drank as much as we could. Chica moved toward

her bowl and slid it under the neck of the bottle. Very smart! She was gathering water for later. I followed suit. I waited while the water filled her bowl. As soon as hers was filled, I nudged the bottleneck over my bowl. There the water continued pouring out until it filled my bowl. Unfortunately, there was no way to make it stop.

Finally, the water ceased pouring out on its own; however, we could still see water inside. We decided to leave the rest of the water in the bottle. We would have it for later. I still felt a little sick and not very hungry. Warm meat was not good for us. Warm milk wasn't either. Water was what we knew and what we would drink forever.

The sun was overhead in the sky. We were both feeling better. As I finished drinking my water, Chica was spending her time trying to open the door to our dog food. The old man kept the bag behind the cabinet door. When trying to nose it open didn't work, Chica started headbutting the door. After three headbutts, her perseverance paid off. She was able to push her nose into the space between the door and the cabinet and force it open. I saw an opportunity and jumped on the bag of dog food, pulling it over onto the floor. Dry, hard pellets spilled everywhere. We knew this food. We lapped up the scattered pieces, chewing loudly as we filled our bellies again.

The old man lay still, his eyes closed. Chica and I both started to lick his face once more. Maybe it was our way of checking to see if he really was dead, or maybe it was our way of saying goodbye. He was cold and didn't smell like himself. I knew it was time. We could not stay here. The old man needed Maria. There were animals living in the desert that would smell him and maybe try to take him. I loved the old man. I wanted Maria to take him, not the wild creatures in the desert. We needed a plan. He had saved us from being a meal for desert animals. We needed to save him from the same fate.

"Chica, we must go and find Maria. She will come back here and help the old man. He would want us to do that for him."

Chica nodded in agreement. I continued. "The old man has taken us to her casa many times. He would always drive us on the old dirt road into town. If we follow that road, we will eventually find the town. Once we are there, we can look for Maria's house."

Chica nodded in agreement. Then I added, "All we need to do is follow the road into town. We need to go soon, Chica. Drink a little more water. Eat a little more food."

We both did as I said. I knew food would not be a problem on our journey since we could always eat lagartos. Water was something else.

"No matter what happens, Chica, we have each other." Of course, I wasn't thinking of coyotes when I said that. "Follow me."

I led the way with Chica close behind. I pushed on the screen door with my front paws until it opened and watched as it closed. I turned and looked back. Wishing he were standing in the doorway, I barked, "Goodbye, old man. We will find Maria and bring her back to you."

As Chica fell in step with me heading down the road, I looked confident, but I felt scared. I could not show fear because Chica needed me to be strong so she would be strong. After everything that had happened, I was amazed we could be so brave. We did not have time to feel sorry for ourselves. We had lost a wonderful man whose joyfulness was felt every day. He was our light in our dark times and saved Chica and me from death. I loved him. Chica loved him. He was our family. Now we needed to find the rest of his family. We would do that for him. The old man would want Maria and his grandchildren here.

The sun was setting, and darkness began to surround us. The dirt road was dusty, but we knew that Maria would always come by this road to see the old man. Whenever the old man took us to town in his truck, he would also drive on this road. *Stay on the road or close to it* is what I told myself so we could find Maria.

"We need to find a place to sleep before we lose all light," I told Chica. "The place we find must be close to the road we're following.

I see a place over there by the rocks. It's a perfect spot for us. Keep your eyes open."

I led the way to the rocks, sniffing the air and moving cautiously. Nothing. I could smell nothing strange or dangerous in the air. We slowly moved to the spot. I backed up to the rock and lay down. Chica moved in and curled up against me. We both felt safe as the darkness surrounded us. Familiar sounds of the night could be heard in the distance. We were both so tired. We may have lost the old man whom we loved greatly, but we still had each other, and we had a purpose. Somehow, I knew everything would be all right.

"Sleep, Chica," I said. "The old man is watching over us. I'm sure of it." We gave in to our exhaustion and fell asleep.

Chapter 9
SEÑOR HISSY

THE NEXT MORNING, I AWOKE feeling the need to relieve myself. Slowly, I rose from my spot with Chica still asleep and moved cautiously behind the large rocks we had slept against. Chica must have felt my absence and called out, "Napoli, where are you?"

"I am relieving myself, which I am sure you will need to do as well." Chica got up and joined me behind the rocks.

It took me a few minutes to realize where we were. Once the sun was visible in the morning sky, I could see we weren't at the ranch. Then it hit me. The old man was gone, and Chica and I were going to town to find his daughter, Maria.

"Napoli, are you hungry?" Chica asked me.

"Yes, Chica," I responded as I kicked dirt over my fresh pee.

"What do you think we should do for food?"

"What we have done when we've had to. Let's start looking for lagartos."

Chica was standing and sniffing the air. I stretched one more time and looked around. I started to walk, and Chica fell in step behind me. We moved in the direction of the road. The road would take us to town, and it would take us to Maria. I did not want to lose sight of it.

Suddenly, I saw movement in the distance. Chica saw it too and began to run toward it, with no thought of what it might be. I followed her. As we got closer, I smelled a vile smell. I knew it was dangerous. I had smelled it before. I started to run as fast as I could to catch up to Chica. She was almost on top of the creature. Then its tail began to shake. It shook, rattled, and began to coil.

Chica was surprised by its movement and stood back. As I came upon her, the snake was coiled, and its head was pulling upward in the coil. Chica did not know the danger. I had encountered this creature before when I was with Panchito hunting.

Panchito said my name in almost a whisper. "Napoli, come with me now. We need to leave here." Panchito then turned to me with a serious look on his face. "Napoli, that snake is extremely dangerous."

I quickly opened my mouth wide and placed it over Chica's small head. She was trapped. I would not let her get any closer. I was hurting her, but I knew it was for her own good.

Señor Hissy pushed his tongue in and out. I wasn't sure if he thought he might be able to take both of us, but I was not going to waste another second finding out. I remembered how the rabbit had reacted to the snake's bite the day I was with Panchito, and decided it was time to turn and run.

I began to drag Chica by the head until she understood we needed to get away. Once I knew she was calming down and following my lead, I released her.

Chica followed me farther away from the ticking snake. His hideous eyes followed our movements. Señor Hissy was angry. Most of all, I think, he was very hungry. Chica let out a bark in Señor Hissy's direction. What Chica didn't realize was that she would have probably made a nice meal for that slithery creature.

She continued to bark when out of nowhere another snake appeared. It was huge and very long. Señora Black and White had black and white stripes all over her body. She slithered past us. It was obvious she was not interested in us but was focused on Señor Hissy.

Chica and I backed up and watched this scary-looking creature as it made its way toward Señor Hissy. We could hear the rattle from the Señor shaking more, but Señora Black and White was not frightened off. She kept coming, ready to do battle with Señor Hissy.

Chica and I were frozen in our spot. We could not take our eyes off the scene in front of us. Señor Hissy made the first move. With his mouth open, he struck at the Señora. Señora Black and White moved her head quickly to the right. Señor Hissy lashed out again. This time, the massive snake moved her head to the other side and clamped down on Señor Hissy's neck right behind his head. I was sure Señor Hissy was surprised by this move. He began to flail his tail. As we watched, we could see that the Señora was not shaken. She clamped down harder on Señor's neck. The flailing stopped. Señora Black and White stood with Señor Hissy's head drooping from her mouth.

As we watched, wondering what would happen next, the Señora showed us. We stood in awe as Señora Black and White began to swallow Señor Hissy's head. We couldn't believe our eyes. Why didn't she get sick? It looked like this was her food, and after eating the head, she continued to swallow Señor Hissy's body.

I had escaped that menacing Señor Hissy twice, and Chica had now escaped him once. At this point, I felt we had seen enough of both snakes.

"Come, Chica. This is only making me hungry. Let's find our food."

And just then, a slender lagarto popped out of the bushes and began to run. It didn't take long for me to catch it and selfishly eat it.

"The next one is for you, Chica."

And so, it was. We filled our bellies until we could no longer eat. Thank goodness lizards were always plentiful in the desert. We would never starve.

The sun was almost above us, and we understood the importance of our task ahead. Onward we walked on the road, away from Señor Hissy and our new hero, Señora Black and White.

Chapter 10
SEÑORITA STINGING TAIL

THE DAY SEEMED UNUSUALLY LONG as we walked in the hot sun. The air felt dry, and the warm air of the desert was the only thing I could smell. Chica and I were having no trouble chasing and catching tiny four-legged animals for our meals. We would work together, digging out lizards, chasing them down, and sharing each one that we caught. We were also careful not to encounter another Señor Hissy in the brush. Our eyes were always on the lookout for any movement. We had a mission, and we didn't need any problems to stop us from finding Maria.

It was during one of our hunts for food that we encountered a new and somewhat dangerous situation. Chica saw a very fat lagarto dashing from the bushes and across the desert floor. She began to run after it before I could get my legs to follow. The lagarto ran into some brush and disappeared. Chica ran into the same brush, saw a small hole, and began digging. I watched her dig. I am sure she was thinking the lagarto was in that hole. Unfortunately, instead of a fat lagarto popping out, a creature the size of the lizard slowly rose with its tail above its head. Chica lunged for it. The creature was having none of it and shot its tail in the direction of Chica's cheek.

For a second, I could see that Chica was unnerved by the action and was getting ready to bite down when she stopped and pulled back. I barked. "What's wrong, Chica?"

By the time I reached her, Chica was rubbing her cheek across the dirt, whimpering, and shaking her head back and forth. I didn't know what to do to help her. I just watched her rubbing her cheek in the dirt.

I could see the creature that had stung Chica quickly walk away, back to its hole, and disappear. Chica seemed to be in a great deal of pain.

"Chica, what are you feeling?" I asked her.

Chica lifted her head from the dirt. "Oh, Napoli. My face is on fire."

I noticed something was greatly wrong. One side of her face appeared as though two or three lizards were stuffed in her cheek. In seeing how her cheek had reacted, I realized Chica's encounter with Señorita Stinging Tail had been dangerous.

I proceeded to lick her cheek but that did not help. Her little body began to shake, and her eyes filled with tears.

"Oh, Chica. Señorita Stinging Tail has hurt you. I don't know what to do to help you." I lowered my eyes for a moment. "Chica, we need to find water. We need it for drinking and for your cheek."

I barked to Chica to follow me as I proceeded to find water. I could tell by how slowly she was moving that she was not feeling well.

Down the road we walked. The sun was overhead, causing any shadows from the tall cactuses to be smaller than usual. Chica tried to stop many times and finally spoke up. "Napoli, I am so tired. I know I need water, but I want to stop and rest. I feel sick. Please, Napoli. Don't push me anymore. Let me lie here while you find water. Please?"

I understood and was more scared than ever. I walked Chica to a nearby cluster of rocks and checked them out. No Señor Hissy?

No Señorita Stinging Tail? It was safe. I nosed her against the rock, licked her cheek again, and set off to find water.

As I moved inland, I could see a herd of cows grazing on the bushes. Farther in, I could see more cows gathered around what I hoped was water. As I got closer, the cows just looked up at me and continued to drink. It was water—a small watering hole in the middle of nowhere. I walked over and began to quench my thirst. It was cold and it was good, and most of all, the cows did not seem to mind that I was sharing it.

I ran back to let Chica know. As soon as I got close to where she lay, I started to bark for her to get up and come. She did not move. I barked louder. Slowly, she raised her head and looked over at me. Her one eye was shut from the swelling, while her other eye searched my face.

"Chica! You need to get up and follow me. I have found water. It's cold and good. You need to put your face in it and drink to fill your belly. I need you to get up, now!"

Unsteadily, Chica began to rise. She had difficulty balancing and fell over. Struggling to stand once more, I saw her fall again. I wanted to help. I realized I could not pick her up like a puppy, but I could assist her.

I clamped down on the back of her neck and started to walk her to the watering hole. We would have to stop every few feet just for me to rest and grab on again. Chica was having trouble breathing. It seemed labored and difficult for her to take in air. "What did Señorita Stinging Tail do to you? What is happening to your body? Please, Chica, I need you to get well. You are my only friend. You are my sister."

I felt more strength in my grip. I grabbed onto her neck and dragged her. The water was getting closer. We passed the cows as they watched me and heard Chica whimper. *Just a few more feet,* I thought.

As we approached the watering hole, there were now three cows drinking. I think the scene of my dragging a whimpering animal made them nervous. They raised their heads and walked away, bumping into each other. *Good! More space for us,* I thought.

I dropped Chica next to the water. The ground was wet, and her white fur became very muddy. I pushed her toward the water and barked at her. "Chica! Put your burning face in the water, now! The water will put out the fire."

Chica could barely raise her small head, but she managed to inch her way closer and set her cheek into the cool water. She scooted back and began to drink. Then she did a very clever thing: she lay her swollen cheek on the cool mud and let it rest there.

What a great idea! Chica had the wet ground sticking to her swollen cheek. The mud from the slobbering cows was nice and thick. She lay there relaxed and seemingly better.

"Chica, stay here! I will catch us some food. You need to eat. Drink and fill your belly full of water. I will be back!" And off I ran.

Lizard after lizard shot out from their hiding places. Only one bite from me, and they were dead. I would bring each lizard back to Chica. She would raise her muddied face and try to eat. It was difficult, but at least she tried.

Finally, by the fourth lizard I brought back, I noticed she wasn't eating them anymore. She had finished most of the first, but the second and third just sat where I had left them. I proceeded to eat the fourth myself. Chica was tired, but at least she had eaten, and she had water.

I could see we were not going to be traveling anywhere until her swollen face got smaller. I knew it would be important to stay close to the mud and the water for a while, but maybe not this close; I wouldn't want a cow to step on her. I managed to help her over to some brush growing next to two large rocks. I checked it out to make sure there were no dangerous creatures. When I sniffed the air, the cows were the only thing I could smell. I also moved the remaining lizards close to her face in case she got hungry in the night.

"Napoli, I need to sleep," Chica said to me. "I am so tired. Por favor. Let me sleep. I really don't want to walk anymore."

I lacked the strength to drag her down the road farther. I could only hope that she would get stronger, and I knew that water was part of what she would need while getting better. Nodding, I agreed that sleep was our only choice right now.

As Chica lay there still, I observed big black birds with red faces circling overhead. A few of the crazy ones landed and ventured closer to Chica. I wondered if they were after Chica, or were they after the lizards I had left for Chica? They did not see me off to the side. The minute I raced from behind the bush, they flew away. "Be gone, you ugly black birds."

To my disappointment, they did not leave the area. They managed to sit outside of our invisible safe zone. I watched them fly around, land, and stare in the direction of Chica. There seemed to be more of them on the ground than in the air. I had a feeling they would maintain their distance as long as I was eyeing them. They didn't seem brave enough to deal with me and my teeth, which I bared in their direction.

"There is no meat here for you to eat! Go away! Look elsewhere for food," I barked.

Were they thinking that Chica would become their dinner, or were they just interested in the dead lizards by her? I had always seen these birds in the sky but didn't know much about them. "Go away, black birds! Chica needs her sleep!"

As the group of birds watched Chica, I felt I needed to do something. It was getting dark, and I wanted to know their every move. I made the decision that I would sleep in front of Chica. If those birds tried to peck at her body, I would know and wake to defend her.

Once more, I dragged her to the cool water and forced her to drink. I had her sink her cheek into the mud that banked the water. Then I dragged her back to the rock and took my position with her against the rock and me pressed against and on top of her. I couldn't see the birds at that moment. I wasn't sure if the surrounding darkness had shooed them away or if they were waiting in the brush. Whatever the case, I was making the right choice. My Chica would be safe between the rock and me. I just hoped that we would be safe so close to a watering hole and in the darkness. The good news for us that evening was the moon was exceptionally large, so at least I would be able to see around us.

"Go to sleep, Chica. Get your strength back! I need you to be Chica again. The old man needs us to find Maria! You will be better tomorrow. I just know it."

With those last words, I found myself dozing off. I was falling to sleep and couldn't stop myself. "Goodnight, Chica. Get well, por favor."

Chapter 11
SEÑORA DONKEY AND BABY

THE NEXT MORNING, I WAS awakened by the sound of birds cawing. As I looked down, I realized that Chica was not in front of me as she usually was when we slept. Turning my head and seeing her behind me, I nudged her to wake up. She didn't move. She lay perfectly still. For a second, I felt my heart race and my breathing stop.

"Chica! Are you awake?" I said those words louder than I intended. Maybe my worry about losing her came rushing out in my volume.

"Chica! Wake up! We must find Maria! Wake up!" My voice sounded fearful.

"Why are you yelling, Napoli? I'm awake, and I'm feeling better."

My joy began to show as I quickly moved toward Chica and started licking the top of her head.

"You're okay, Chica?" I felt like crying when she nodded. "Are you hungry? Can I find you something to eat? You need to drink some water first."

"Slow down, Napoli. Yes, I feel better. Yes, I am hungry. And yes, I am ready for some water." Chica almost sounded like her old self.

I watched as she slowly rose from her side. She fell back a little before she took her first step. The swelling on her face had gone down. Her eye was almost the same size as the other. She wobbled as she walked to the watering hole. She wasn't strong enough yet. Water and food would help her.

I knew that we would walk slower today. She had been near death. Between Señorita Stinging Tail hurting her and the black birds pestering her, my poor Chica had had a harrowing experience. It would take time before she felt like herself again.

"I need to relieve myself and find you some very fat lagartos to satisfy your hunger," I told her. "While I'm gone, drink lots of water, and keep your eyes open. You have been through a lot, mi amiga. I will be back in no time with plenty of food for you."

Chica nodded and looked around at the cows in the area. They seemed to be waiting for their turn at the watering hole. Before I left, I sniffed the air for anything that might present a danger to her. Seeing nothing and smelling nothing, I proceeded on my way to find food for us. I could hear her slurping the water as I left.

My Chica was all right. My happiness was showing. I felt like I could fly. At that moment, two very fat lagartos popped out from the bush in front of me. "Ahhh. You make my life easier. Keep running together. I will sweep you both up in one bite." And I did.

Returning to Chica, I found her resting against the cluster of rocks. She was sunning with half her face covered in dry mud.

"Chica! Look what I brought you, nice fat lizards for your stomach. Eat them slowly."

Chica sat up and began to eat. She chewed the first lizard, starting from the middle and moving her chomping to its tail. She purposely avoided the head. She started on the second lizard in the same way.

I told Chica, "Put your face in the water and move your head around. You need to clean off the mud on your cheek in case we see Maria today. She will not recognize you with a muddy face." Chica stared at me, nodding. "While you're in there, drink more water. Water heals everything."

Chica did everything I suggested. By the time she was done, the sun was almost above us. We were getting a late start, but at least we were finally ready.

As we slowly left our safe place, we could hear something in the brush ahead of us. It was the sound of a donkey, but this donkey was in a lot of pain. As we approached the bushes, we saw why. Señora Donkey was lying on the dirt, breathing hard. Her stomach was exceptionally large and very round. I knew that she was about to give birth. Chica and I kept our distance so as not to startle her and focused on her stomach as it moved up and down very slowly. She let out another painful cry. It was at that moment I could see something moving in the bushes to her side.

Chica was now aware of something as she sniffed the air. I smelled it too. Chica nervously moved back and forth. The bushes circling Señora Donkey were rustling. There was not one enemy but four. As Señora Donkey cried out again, the shadows in the bushes made their presence known. Slowly, and in an almost crawling formation, four faces began to peer out. I suspected the four-pack were more interested in what the mother donkey would be passing than in the mother herself.

I am not a fool, but I knew I had to do something other than run. I remembered the coyotes from when Chica and I had almost died. Even though I was bigger than the coyotes that had attacked us, I was sure it was only because of the old man that I was alive today. I wasn't so worried about myself as I was for little Chica and for the baby donkey that would soon be born.

Instinctively, I growled in the pack's direction. I bared my teeth and growled deeper. The coyotes now knew that they were not alone. The biggest of the four stood up, startling Señora Donkey. It seemed like she realized what was happening and rose quickly. I sensed she instinctively knew she needed to act before her baby arrived.

I started barking, and so did Chica. "Chica! Stay close to me," I said. "I don't trust those four. If they can, they may try for you as well."

Chica knew that what I was saying made sense. Besides, she could bark menacingly, but she was not sure of her strength yet. She did as she was told and barked like I had never heard her bark before.

Señora Donkey saw us. At first, she seemed confused. Were we trying to harm her too? Chica and I moved in closer to the donkey and barked louder at the coyotes. They began to separate, putting us in the middle of their circle. I turned to the donkey and barked.

Señora Donkey seemed to understand what I needed her to do. Her head followed my barking and lined the coyotes up in front of me. I angled myself so that two of the coyotes were directly behind her hind legs.

My barks became stronger. I could only hope she realized what I was trying to say to her. "Kick, Señora! Kick those ugly creatures. Kick, with the strength you have left. Kick now!"

Señora Donkey acted as though she spoke dog and kicked her hind legs with every bit of her strength. One, then two coyotes screamed out as they were tossed like rocks into the dirt. Each one fell on its side, yelping in pain. Instead of coming at us again, the two limped off in the opposite direction.

The other two coyotes watched and began to move forward, avoiding the donkey's strong hind legs. To my surprise, Señora Donkey stood up on her back legs and came down hard on the larger of the two remaining coyotes. The smaller coyote could see that its friend was hurt. The sudden turn of events sent the two coyotes fleeing the area, one of them hobbling. Señora Donkey, with her giant belly, had done it! She shook her head up and down and tilted it side to side. It must have taken all her strength to kick her hind legs with such force, then to stand upright on those same legs. She was amazing!

I noticed that Señora Donkey became perfectly still. I wondered if all the excitement had worn her out. Then I noticed her eyes became wider, and one eye on the side of her head looked directly into my eyes. From the look on her face, I knew Señora Donkey was getting ready to drop a baby from her backside. It was happening soon. Chica and I backed up and watched in total disbelief. How this mamá could fight for survival one minute and give birth the next was something to behold.

Señora Donkey moved in place, turning slightly so her backside was more visible from where we were standing. The baby was showing now. For a second, it seemed to be stuck. There was no movement and no sound. I wondered what I should do to help her. Chica and I continued to be still as we watched. Then rather quickly, it all happened. Out popped the baby, landing in the dirt with a thud.

The thud caused Señora Donkey to jump forward, away from the sound. After calming down, she turned around in the direction of her baby. Seconds later, moving forward and licking the baby's large head, she nudged it with her nose. The baby appeared to respond. Chica and I almost started laughing watching this newborn trying to stand on its shaky legs. After a few tries, and with enough coaxing from the mamá, the baby stood, then moved to her side. Instinctively, it stretched out its neck to feed under her belly.

What a lovely, peaceful scene. Watching the baby feed made me think of my Mamá. This scene could have been a disaster if not for Chica and me and Señora Donkey's powerful kicks. It was her good fortune that we came along at just the right time.

In the quiet, I could hear other donkeys in the distance, and knew Señora Donkey needed to be with them. I barked for her and her baby to follow us. Chica was surprised by my bark. "You know the saying, Chica, that there is safety in numbers? I heard the old man say that once when we were hunting. Well, I suspect that coyotes are smart enough to stay away from herds of donkeys no matter how empty their bellies are feeling. The baby will stand a better chance of survival with many donkeys to defend it."

Mamá and baby willingly followed Chica and me along the trail until we caught up to the other donkeys. Without wasting a moment, the two proceeded to join the herd. Walking in their direction, Señora Donkey briefly looked back. I imagined she was thanking Chica and me. We watched as her baby followed closely behind her and moved to the safety of the group.

"Come on, Chica. We need to make up time. We have lost a better part of the day, and we must find Maria. Vamos, Chica! Vamos!"

"Napoli," Chica asked, "since we saved the baby donkey from the coyotes just like the old man saved us from them, do you think Señora Donkey thinks of us like we thought of the old man?"

"Actually, Chica, if the mamá donkey had not been there, we might have become coyote dinner. We didn't do so well the last time we encountered them. She stopped those coyotes. In a way of thinking, she saved us."

Chica thought about what I said and nodded. "Yikes, Napoli."

"As the old man would say, things have a way of working out."

We picked up our pace and headed in the direction of the road. I couldn't help but smile when I thought of Chica having recovered from being so sick and then our saving the baby donkey. What a day! It was all good. And I was on the road again with my best friend.

Chapter 12
HISSSSSSSSSSSS

Chica and I slowed our pace. We were both complaining of hunger and thirst. I had not seen a lizard since we left our donkey friends miles back. Nor had we seen any water for quite some time. I had let my mind drift with memories of the old man, his smiles, and his singing floating in and out of my thoughts.

We still had plenty of light, and knowing we weren't going to find water on the dirt road, I decided we would veer off and search through the brush. Narrow paths surrounded the trees and bushes away from the road. Chica was the most cautious of the cactuses we came upon. She kept a courteous distance from each one we saw.

We had been walking inland for what seemed like a very long time when we happened upon a tall clump of rocks. It came to me that if I could get to the top of that cluster, I would have the best vantage point to find water.

"Follow me, Chica! I need to climb to the top of those rocks. You wait at the bottom for me. I am hoping to see water or vacas from up there."

I walked over to the rocks with Chica following me and jumped onto the lowest rock. Chica positioned herself as lookout on the ground. From there, I stepped on ascending rocks until I was on the highest one. As I stood and looked from my rock platform, I could see a small herd of vacas in the distance. They were far enough away that I couldn't smell them or hear them.

"Chica, I see cows. I have a feeling they are gathered around water. Let's go there. If we are lucky, we will drink, and then I will find us food."

Chica nodded and waited for me to jump down and lead the way. She followed behind me, sniffing the air as we walked.

The vacas sensed us coming. As we got closer, they began to moo and groan. When we entered their area, they slowly moved away, circling each other. Once I knew they were no threat to us, I looked over the area and spotted a small watering hole, just right for two very thirsty perras.

Chica bolted for the water without a care in the world. I was more cautious as I moved in behind her. When Chica reached the hole, she dived in belly-first. It didn't take long for her to fill her stomach with water and cool her fur.

"Chica, stand here and guard as I take my turn drinking. Keep your eyes open. Understood?" I looked at her for a response.

Chica nodded and took a position behind where I was standing while I dipped my tongue into the murky water. *Ahh!* It tasted good even though it looked like mud. *Ahh!* My belly was feeling full, with only enough room for a couple of fat lagartos.

"Okay, Chica. How many lagartos can you eat? Huh? Two lagartos, three, six? I have room for maybe three very fat lagartos. Come on. Let's hunt together. Keep up with me."

Chica wagged her tail and stood in my shadow. I perused the area, aware that lizards would not be hiding where the cows were standing. They would have run off before the cows got there. I looked where I saw the most hiding places. I walked slowly to the brush on the opposite side of where the vacas stood and circled the area carefully to not startle our dinner. Unfortunately, hunting seemed to take longer than usual. *Where are you, lagartos? Where are you hiding?*

"Chica, help me secure the area. Stay here while I head to the other side. I will flush them out by zigzagging into our space. Surely there must be something to eat in this brush."

Chica stayed put while I walked across the way. I knew lizards had to be here somewhere since there was so much greenery and they loved to hide in bushes. Once I was in position, I signaled Chica to watch for food. I began to walk into the brush, paying careful attention to any movement at all. I was aware it could be dangerous, but my hope was to find a few fat lizards.

I stepped into a cluster of green shrubs. The minute I put my second paw in the cluster, three lagartos rushed from where they had been safely hiding. One small one headed toward Chica, and two fat ones separated and scurried in opposite directions from me. Without a moment's hesitation, I ran after the fattest one, thinking maybe his girth might slow him down. I was right. He moved toward a hole in the ground and tried to scurry in and away from me.

Señor Lagarto, you will never fit. Bad choice! And I placed my paw on his tail and grabbed him with my teeth before he could break away. *Ahhh.* I couldn't wait. I began to chew. He was so tender and just what I needed. When I looked up, I noticed that Chica had caught her own dinner. She was chewing on the smaller lagarto. We were both victorious. It was a beginning. We caught a few more until we could not swallow one more piece.

Chica found shade by a cactus. I joined her. A small siesta was in order. We both knew it had already been a tiring day. Just a small nap would get us ready again to find Maria. Just a small nap, until the sun was no longer beating on us. Just a small …

"Chica, wake up! We are sleeping our day away. Let's go, muchacha! We need to find Maria. The old man needs us to find her."

Chica raised her head slowly and licked her paws. She walked to the murky watering hole and lapped up some water. I followed her with the same intention. *Water!*

"Follow close behind me, Chica. We'll head back to the road."

It took us a while to find our way back. I hadn't realized how far we had veered away from it. Our plan had always been to use the dirt road as our trail to Maria's house in town. Her car would have traveled in this direction since there were no other choices. Time was turning out to be our problem.

"Chica, we've had a lot of diversions along the way. I have lost track of how many times the sun has risen and set on this journey. We should be close. We need to make up the time we've lost."

We pushed on down the road, only stopping when necessity called. I looked up occasionally throughout the day to see the sun in a new position in the sky. It was low now. This was the time when the old man would call us for dinner. He loved to have us eat when he ate. He would talk to us while he ate. We were his family. He was the best family I had ever known. *Please wait, old man. We are getting help for you. We are bringing Maria to you. Please forgive us for taking so long.* I blinked my eyes and cleared the tears.

"Napoli, isn't it getting near dinner and time to sleep again?" Chica looked at me with huge eyes, waiting for me to agree.

"Yes, Chica. It is time to eat and sleep once more. I think we look for vacas and find water. There is so much green around here, which is a good sign. Let's walk to those rocks in the distance and climb to the top. We'll be able to see from there."

Chica followed my lead. I was careful where I stepped, and both of us constantly sniffed the air, stopping occasionally to check for unusual sounds. Chica did what I did. It was almost funny to see her copy my movements. We doubled our safety!

When we reached the rocks, I jumped up on the first large rock in the trio. Chica was having some difficulty getting to my level, so I bent over while she stood up with her paws against the rock. I grabbed the back of her neck. With all my might, I pulled her up to me. After realizing she was okay with this action, I jumped to the next rock, pulling her up gently with my teeth.

"Napoli, I like being up high. I can see far."

"I know, Chica. It is a beautiful view from here."

We were both taking in the desert colors and shadows when I noticed movement in the grass ahead of us. "Look over there! I see something."

Chica turned to where I was staring. "Napoli, is it a vaca or a hungry coyote? What is it now?"

"I know, Chica. Living in the desert seems to be about danger at every turn, or survival of the fittest. Whatever it is, we have each other. We will come through this too."

We both watched as the grass separated in a zigzag pattern. I had a feeling I knew what it was, but I wanted to see to be sure. We waited and watched.

Coming out into the clearing with its forked tongue moving in and out of its mouth, and the triangular head moving side to side, this was the longest, thinnest snake I had ever seen. By the looks of it, I supposed that it was very hungry; maybe it hadn't eaten in a while. Señor Hissy was rattling its tail in our direction. This was what Panchito called a dangerous snake. Panchito once told me that the desert was filled with these dangerous snakes. Chica and I had been lucky since we had escaped the other Señor Hissy. Señora Black and White had saved us then. I was hoping our luck hadn't run out.

We watched as this long Señor Hissy moved into the clearing by our rocks. Maybe he wasn't aware of us, but his tongue was moving so quickly in and out of his mouth. I wasn't sure, but I wondered if maybe that movement helped him find food.

Chica moved closer to me. I knew she was scared. When you are as small as she is, you must think that anything larger could eat you.

"It's okay, Chica. We are high up from Señor Hissy. He can't reach us up here," I told her.

But as we watched, Señor Hissy started toward the rocks. With his tongue flipping in and out, he began to extend his body up the first rock. *What? He can climb rocks?* I asked myself. We watched him as he reached the height of the first rock and began sliding his head over the ledge, moving toward the second rock, which we were perched on.

I felt panic building up in my chest. "Chica, I am going to move us up one more rock. Hang on!"

I clamped down on Chica's neck. I saw Señor Hissy starting up through the cracks in the second rock. I looked up where I needed to go. That was a large jump for me, and carrying Chica was going to make it harder. Señor Hissy was getting closer, with his tongue moving faster in and out. I knew I had to make this happen. I had to save Chica and myself from that awful creature. As I focused on the top of the third rock, I leaned back on my hind legs. I felt energy—or was it fear?—filling my chest. Everything was dependent on my leap. I growled a warning, hoping Señor Hissy would acknowledge it by turning and going back down, but it didn't seem to matter. He was coming. He must have been very hungry.

I took a deep breath through my nose while I held Chica by my teeth and looked down one more time. Then I focused on the ledge above me. With everything I was feeling in my body, I jumped into the air. I felt Chica's weight as I was airborne and worried about what would happen if I missed and fell back onto Señor Hissy. My body was shaking. I closed my eyes. *Let me make it!*

I felt the rock and opened my eyes. Half my body and most of Chica's was on the rocky ledge. When I released her from my grip, Chica scrambled away from me. She was safe, but I could feel myself slipping.

"Napoli! Please try harder," Chica said. "You need to claw with your back legs. I do not know how to help you."

"Chica, stand back! I don't want to knock into you."

Chica quickly moved to the edge. I started clawing with my back paws. My head was down, and my front paws were slipping on the ledge. I raised my eyes, looking ahead for anything to help me boost myself onto the rock. Señor Hissy was almost to the second level. How was that possible?

"Claw your way up, Napoli! Come on, you need to do this." Chica's voice was fearful as she pleaded with me to join her.

I clawed harder. My front and back paws began to gain ground. I was moving closer to where Chica was standing, and even though my back legs still dangled, I knew I was almost there.

"Napoli, you did it!" Chica exclaimed once I was safe beside her. "You got both of us up here safely. Muchas gracias, my dear friend."

"I can only hope this is enough," I said with a slightly relieved bark.

We both looked over the edge. Señor Hissy's ugly face was now moving around on the second ledge. He was looking for us. I was too large for him, but I knew that Chica would probably be just right. I was sure Chica knew it too. She huddled closer, waiting for me to come up with another plan. We could not stay here all night. We were hungry and thirsty, and the sun was now setting. Even if Señor Hissy could not climb to the third level, how were we going to get out of this?

"Napoli. What is that coming this way?"

As I looked in the direction Chica was looking, I saw a familiar bird—one that I had seen race by us many times on our journey. It was a funny-looking bird that appeared to be wearing a feather hat. It was skinnier than the chickens back at the old man's house and had long feathers jutting out of its backside. I had never seen them fly, but they were always running around in a hurry. They had never approached us before; however, I thought this one was going to be different.

"Chica, it's one of those funny-looking birds we have seen running by us in the desert. I wonder what she's up to."

We both looked down at the Señora. What could she be planning? Then we saw it.

"I think that crazy Señora is pecking at Señor Hissy's body, Napoli. Is she loco? Why would she do that?"

We watched as this funny-looking bird pecked fearlessly at Señor Hissy. To our relief, Señor Hissy began to pull away from the second rock. He dropped down to confront the irritating intruder. Maybe he thought that this bird was a far easier meal than the perras on the rocks.

From our lofty position, Chica and I saw this brave bird standing and staring at the coiled serpent. I wondered if she faced such danger for sport. Was this just fun for her? We watched from the top of our rock, feeling very safe for the moment.

Señor Hissy, from his coiled position, struck out at Señora Brave Bird. Our feathered friend did not back down as Señor Hissy struck out again with his mouth wide open and his fangs showing. Señora Brave Bird was quick and positioned herself in front of Señor Hissy. The angry snake struck out, missed, struck out again, and missed again. The brave bird moved quickly to the right. Another strike from the snake, and a miss. The snake's tail was rattling louder and faster. Then the Señora hopped behind Señor Hissy. No strike. Instead, the Señor seemed confused.

Señora Brave Bird—with her long, thin beak—clamped down on the neck of Señor Hissy. *Bam!* Her beak gripped the neck of this dangerous snake. We watched as the snake's body uncoiled and coiled over and over. She tightened her hold and began slamming Señor Hissy's head to the ground. Once, twice, three times, Señor Hissy's head hit the dirt. With the head dangling from her mouth, Señora Brave Bird moved around, not letting the scaly skin of Señor Hissy touch her. She was so quick on her skinny bird legs.

Chica and I watched closely, not believing the bravery of this funny-looking bird. Did she know how dangerous a game she was playing? We watched. We hoped. We wanted the Señora to win this battle.

"Chica, I think Señor Hissy has stopped moving. I think the Señora has killed him."

We both stared as the lifeless body of Señor Hissy fell from the mouth of Señora Brave Bird. She stood over him, pecking his body and making sure he was dead. Chica and I sat on the top rock, wanting to leave but not wanting to startle the funny-looking bird. We watched as she picked up the head of Señor Hissy and began to slowly swallow it. She was eating this snake as easily as Chica and I ate lagartos, except we would bite into them. She was swallowing the snake whole. This was no game. This was food for her. This was her dinner.

We sat mesmerized by the scene before us. In some ways, it reminded me of Señora Black and White and how she swallowed the first Señor Hissy. And here we were, watching the same thing again, but this time, a funny-looking bird was eating that scary, skinny snake. She made it look easy. I realized just how hungry I was when I began wondering what Señor Hissy might taste like.

Before our very eyes, she devoured that loathsome creature. When she was almost halfway through swallowing the body, we decided to make our exit. Slowly, I helped Chica move down from her perch. When we reached the bottom, we glanced at the unusual scene that was happening next to us and quietly stepped away. We were being careful not to startle Señora Brave Bird.

"Come, Chica," I said. "Let's head out of here and catch some dinner before we lose the light. We might have to wait on finding water until tomorrow, but if we can catch some fat lagartos, they might quench some of our thirst."

We wandered through the brush and located different lagartos, small and large, fleeing from our path. We were successful at catching and eating many. Our bellies full, we headed to the dirt road. The sun was setting, and darkness was replacing the light.

"Chica, we need to find a safe place to sleep. I have had enough excitement for one day."

"Oh, Napoli, how lucky we were that Señora Brave Bird came along when she did. I never want to see another Señor Hissy as long as I live."

"You said that right, Chica. We need to find Maria. We must be getting closer to the town. We'll start walking early tomorrow."

We found a few rocks next to the road. I wasn't sure how safe we were but decided that cuddling with our backs to the rocks might at least get us through the night. We were both tired of this journey. We hoped that tomorrow would prove to be successful. I was thinking about Maria and the old man as Chica and I lay down and fell fast asleep.

Chapter 13
THE DUST-KICKING MONSTERS

HOW MANY DAYS HAS IT *been? How far have we traveled? Where is Maria? What has happened to the old man? We have seen so many things on our journey. Through it all, Chica and I are still together.*

"Napoli! Watch out!" Chica's barking brought me out of my thoughts and back to reality. Two vacas were crossing the road in front of us. I hadn't realized how close they were until Chica barked.

"Napoli, do you think these vacas are walking to water? Maybe we should follow them."

Barking in agreement with Chica, I caught the attention of the second cow, who was not happy to see us and began mooing. In the distance, we heard another moo and then another. Not to scare the two vacas off, we decided to follow from a distance. It wasn't long before they caught up to their plant-eating friends. The herd seemed oblivious to the addition of two more cows. Cautiously, Chica and I watched them, knowing eventually they would find water for us.

Just as we were getting comfortable with our new surroundings, we heard a roaring sound coming from the desert behind us. From that direction, we could see dirt and dust forming clouds in the air. I worried whatever was heading our way was probably not a good thing. Chica and I moved quickly to a cluster of rocks surrounded by brush, placing ourselves behind the formation. From there, we waited to see what that noise was all about.

The vacas were getting nervous. They started mooing louder. A lead cow emerged from the herd and proceeded to walk in the opposite direction of the oncoming noise. The rest of the vacas followed, away from the sound. We stayed hidden, keeping our eyes peeled.

As it neared, I could hear the laughter of people—people wearing funny hats and something over their mouths. The car they were driving was nothing like the old man's car or Maria's. It had no doors or windows, and it was louder than any car I had ever heard before.

The windowless vehicle was driving in the direction of the fleeing cows. Dirt and dust were everywhere, so much so that I had trouble seeing the people in the car. The laughter seemed louder the closer they came. Suddenly, from behind a tree, a deer darted in front of them. I had seen deer at the old man's house before but hadn't seen one since we began our journey.

A woman in the back seat screamed as the car turned sharply to avoid hitting the intruder. The remaining laughter turned to screams as the car hit a rock and rolled over into the arroyo. The voices stopped. The passengers were quiet.

"Chica, there is something wrong. We need to go and see what has happened. Follow me."

I led Chica to the strange-looking car in the arroyo. It was upside down. I could hear moaning sounds but could not see anyone. The people were in trouble, and I was unsure how to help them.

Only a few minutes had passed before we heard another vehicle approaching with more people who were yelling and laughing. They were following the path of the first car but making even more noise. For a moment, I thought they would drive close enough to see the car, but then their car turned a different way on the path. Where they were now, they could not see the accident in the arroyo. Chica and I stood on the hill watching what the second strange-looking car would do next.

It stopped. I listened and waited.

The lady in the back seat spoke up. "Bob, I don't see them anywhere. Which dirt trail do you think they took?"

"I don't know, Susie. I can't hear their buggy, and I don't see their dust cloud."

"Maybe they are nearby waiting for us," the woman named Susie suggested. "Let's call out together. They could have a flat tire or be taking a picture. Come on. Let's yell together."

I watched and listened as the people in the car began yelling, "Rick! Sandy! Janice! Yell if you're here."

"I don't think they're around, or they would have answered. Let's drive further into the desert and see if they are there waiting for us." Bob waited for a response to his suggestion.

The moaning below us grew louder. I knew that if the others drove off, these people would be left in the upside-down car with their injuries. I turned to Chica. "Chica, we need to help these people. Follow me. I'm going after the other car."

I led the way as I had often done, with Chica close behind. The driver of the second car was settling into his seat and getting ready to start the engine. Chica and I stopped at his side of the car and began barking.

"Hey, look at those dogs. What are they doing out here?" Susie smiled at us as she spoke.

Bob responded, "The big one looks upset. Maybe it's rabid or something."

The woman in the passenger seat finally spoke up. "Oh, look at the little dirty white puff ball. So cute."

"Janice, look how small it is next to that huge brown dog. I bet they're thirsty." As Susie spoke, she began to unsnap her seat belt.

"Hold on, Susie. You don't know if those dogs are ill. The way they're barking might indicate they're a little loco. Besides, there are no homes out here. Where'd they come from?" The driver, Bob, was speaking directly to Susie.

The woman named Janice piped in. "I think these dogs were left in the desert to die. I've heard that people will do that sometimes to unload their dogs."

"Oh my God! That's awful, Janice. I hope that isn't the case." Susie redirected her conversation to Chica and me. "Hi, cute puppies. We won't hurt you. I have some water for you." She opened her bottle and poured water into a plastic bag she had picked up off the floor. Slowly, she climbed out of the back seat, opened the bag wide, and carefully set it on the ground next to the car.

The minute Chica saw the water, she raced to it and drank. I was so thirsty, but I wanted to watch and see that these humans were harmless. After seeing their smiles as they were watching Chica drink, I walked over and started to drink as well. That water was cold and tasted wonderful. As soon as my belly was full, I remembered what I had to do and started to bark.

Susie was surprised by my barking and spoke. "Gee, do you think the dog is thanking me for the water?"

The other woman interjected, "I think that big dog wants us to follow her. Look how she leaps in one direction and returns. Maybe she has a master that is hurt and fell somewhere. Bob, I think we should follow."

Bob reluctantly nodded and spoke to us. "All right, girls! You lead the way."

Chica fell in behind me as we started to run to the arroyo. The people maintained a slow speed while following us. I was glad they did not think I was a crazy perra. They trusted me, or maybe they were simply curious. At least they followed. We continued to move toward the spot where the other car had rolled off the small cliff. I stopped, turned, and began barking again.

"Susie, you and Janice wait here. I'll look and see what Lassie wants." Both women laughed at what Bob said. I didn't understand why.

The driver, Bob, walked toward me with a very worried expression. I could tell he was nervous, but he still walked over to where Chica and I were standing. When he reached my side, he looked over the edge. There, he could see the other car, turned upside down.

"Susie, Janice—Rick's car is here. It's upside down, but I can hear sounds coming from it. Hurry!"

The ladies jumped out of the car and ran to Bob. All three of them, followed by Chica and me, slid down the small sandy hillside to the overturned car. Bob started yelling, "Is everyone okay?"

One man's weak voice replied, "Please help me!"

Bob looked around and started crawling into a space in the car. From where I was standing, I could see a passenger in the back who was hanging in his seat belt, unable to reach the buckle. I watched as Bob tried to help him pull it off. The man inside was struggling. I guessed his weight made it difficult to release the belt.

"Terry, I need you to place your head on my back so I can release your belt. I need your weight taken off the belt a little."

I guessed the man in back was Terry since he was the only one who responded. "I'll try. I think I did something to my shoulder. Not sure how it's going to feel when you release me. Maybe you can remain under me so I can carefully pull my shoulder from the strap. What do you think?"

Bob looked up and said, "Can do. Try to push your body off my back. You won't hurt me, so use any means to get your weight off the seat belt so I can release it."

I watched as Bob positioned himself under Terry. Once in place, Bob arched his back. Terry groaned slightly as he shifted his shoulder away from Bob's body, leaning his other shoulder into Bob's back.

"Okay, stay still as I try to release your belt." Bob edged his hand to the release and pressed the button. As soon as Terry's belt opened, it swung back and dangled from the ceiling.

"Egad, Terry, you weigh a ton."

Terry groaned and spoke up. "Oh! My shoulder hurts so much. I think I'm going to have a heck of a time crawling out of here. The pain is excruciating!"

"I'll slide out from under you and move to the open space back here. As soon as I get out of your way, crawl out of the opening on your side. Press your arm tightly against your chest. This should help your shoulder move less. Okay, I'm getting out of your way." Bob slid on his back to the open space under the other seat in the back.

Holding his left arm close to his body, Terry proceeded to shift his weight to the side of Bob's body. Janice and Susie reached in the open window space and helped Terry climb out. Once outside, Bob crawled to the front of the car.

Chica and I were sitting close to the car. We watched as Bob flattened out on the ceiling of the overturned car and spoke up.

"Rick, are you okay?"

The driver moaned a quiet yes, then asked, "Can you get me out of here? I seem to be pinned in my seat."

"I am going to release your seat belt. If you can lighten your weight, that will help me. Maybe use your arms to push off the dashboard?" Bob spoke calmly to keep Rick from panicking.

Rick did as Bob told him, and Bob released his seat belt.

Bob directed Rick out of the windowless space. "You need to go to Sandy's window space. She seems to be unconscious. I plan to get under her and push her up. That way, I can release her belt. She'll be a dead weight on me, so you and the girls need to pull her out. Be careful in case something is broken. I have a first aid kit in the back of my buggy if you need it."

Rick did everything that was asked of him. He and the ladies helped Sandy out of her window space. She wasn't waking up. Rick walked up and knelt beside her, holding her wrist. Then Rick carried her to a shady spot, laying her down. He leaned over her. "I can see her breathing."

He ran up the hill, grabbed a bottle of water and the first aid kit from the other car, and ran back. I watched him as he poured some of the water over Sandy's forehead and hair. She began to move, then cried out. She was alive.

"Sandy, do you have any pain?" Rick's face was inches from hers as he asked the question.

"No, I'm just shaking. One minute, a deer pops out in front of us, and the next minute, you're throwing water in my face." Sandy smiled at everyone.

The group smiled back. Everyone seemed relieved, especially Rick, the driver of the overturned car.

Bob finally crawled out of the window behind Sandy. He stood up and proceeded to dust himself off. He turned to Rick and reached for the water bottle that was used on Sandy and drank.

"Bob, how in the world did you ever find us here in this gully?" Rick looked in Bob's direction as he asked his question.

"Lassie, the big dog, and Little Lassie barked until we followed them. They kind of saved your lives. We were going in the opposite direction to look for your car. Thank goodness they were here."

Susie quickly interjected, "I deserve some credit since I gave them water and suggested we follow them." The sound of groaning came from Terry.

"I would say we're pretty lucky. All in all, it could have been much worse." The group smiled and nodded at what Bob had just said. "However, Terry is hurt and needs to see a doctor. Also, Rick, since you were driving that buggy, you'll need to go to the rental shop and inform them of the accident."

Everyone agreed, grabbed some things out of the overturned car, and started up the hill. Chica and I followed the group. As they reached the other car, they made plans for how all six of them would fit in the seats. It was agreed that Bob would drive, and Terry would sit in the passenger seat and protect his shoulder. Everyone else climbed into the back. Bob assured them he would drive slow enough that the people in back would not need their seat belts.

As they were about to drive off, Susie spoke up. "What about Lassie and Little Lassie? We can't leave them here. After all, they did save some lives today."

Bob hesitated, then replied, "You're right, Susie. We can take them to town with us. Maybe their owner lives there, or just maybe we can help find them a home. Come on, dogs. Climb in front with us."

A ride to town? That would be wonderful! I barked at Chica, and she jumped onto Terry's lap. She fit there comfortably. Bob got out to let me in so I could climb over the driver's seat to the space between the front seats. Once there, I sat down facing the front window. This was a lot better than fighting off animals and drinking muddy water.

Bob pet my head, and Terry held Chica with his good arm. Slowly, we drove toward Maria's town, hopeful that she might be there.

Chapter 14

THE BEGINNING OF THE END

As we drove over the bridge to the town, I could hear familiar sounds in the distance. The old man had driven his red truck over this same route many times with Chica and me on board. Loaded into his cab, with the windows rolled down, he would let us stick our heads outside as he drove. The times when we rode in back, the sounds and smells of the town would bombard us from all sides. The old man knew everyone. Honking and waving were part of our travels with him.

The hospital was close by. The old man had taken us there a couple of times. While he would go in, we would wait in his truck. I knew it was there that we would part ways with these nice people.

The car pulled up to the building with the giant *H* on the front. Bob spoke to Terry and to Janice. "I'm going to let you out here. Janice, go with Terry so he can be attended to while we head over to the rental place and explain to them what happened. You have your phones. Let me know what the diagnosis is regarding his shoulder, and we'll go from there. Okay?"

The two people nodded their heads, and Janice climbed from the back seat to the sidewalk and proceeded to open the small front door on Terry's side. Bob reached over me and picked up Chica while Terry climbed out. That was my cue to jump out behind him. Chica twisted out of Bob's grip and followed me. Once she was on the ground behind me, I turned and barked at the car.

I heard Bob speak to the group. "Well, I guess the Lassies know where they are, so good for them. We need to get over to the rental shop and deal with our dune buggy problem. At least the dogs are no longer in the desert. They helped us and we helped them. Good karma!"

Chica and I started walking. I turned and watched the car with no windows pull away and then pass us. Susie was yelling, "Goodbye!" and "Thank you!" out the back of the car. We both barked back.

"Let's go to Maria's shop," I suggested to Chica. "Maybe she is there."

"What if she's not, Napoli? By now, the animals in the desert are aware of the old man alone in his home."

"You mean dead in his house, Chica."

Chica looked at me for a moment as though thinking about what I had said and finally nodded with her head down. "Yes. Dead, Napoli."

"Let's find Maria."

Chapter 15
VAYA CON DIOS

CHICA BARKED AT MY SUGGESTION. She liked going to Maria's shop. Maria always had clothes in her large front window and treats for us to eat. She was kind to us and seemed happy that we lived with the old man.

Chica and I crossed the street after we left the hospital. I knew which way to go and barked at her to keep up. Cars were slowly going by us, and people were watching us as we walked toward them. We would never hurt them, but we must have looked extra scary from our travels.

As we came to a store with men out front sitting in chairs and talking, one of the men stood up. He saw us and went inside. A second later, he had a broom in his hand.

"Hey, Pedro, grab the little white dog while I beat the big dog out of here."

"Why am I grabbing that dog? It's dirty and so small."

"She's the perfect size for my Lupita. Besides, she is a pedigree and will fetch much money when I sell her future puppies."

"Ahhhhh! Okay, I'll do it, but you better have a cold beer for my effort."

The man with the broom charged at me swinging and yelling. Chica was so confused by the sudden movement and noise that she ran from me and in the direction of the man called Pedro. Pedro blocked her with his feet and bent down and grabbed her. As he pulled her to his chest, she squealed and squirmed and tried to get out of his grip.

Even though the broom hit me a couple of times, I could see what was happening with Chica—my Chica, in the arms of that man. The broom came down hard on my back. I let out a whimper. It hurt so much! If my Chica hadn't been trapped, I would have been out of there and down the road.

Chica heard my cry. I saw Chica do something she had never done before. She turned on the man holding her and bit his chin. The man screamed in pain and threw Chica to the sidewalk. Chica was stunned but got up and ran toward me.

I ran across the street, away from the man with the broom, and Chica ran as fast as her little legs would carry her to my side. The man with the broom ran to his bleeding friend. I could hear many angry words from the bleeding man.

"Chica, we need to run as fast as we can from those hombres. Stay up with me, Chica. I don't know what they'll do if they catch us this time. Run."

Chica stayed close to me as I ran down the street toward Maria's shop. We were far enough away that I thought those men would not chase us. I was wrong. I could see the man who held the broom climb into his car with his bleeding friend climbing in as well. Were they going to come after us? I felt a pang of fear.

The car in the distance started up and moved forward, but instead of coming our way, it turned around and went in the direction from which we came.

"Chica, I don't think they are coming for us. I have a feeling they are heading to the hospital to get the bite fixed."

"Napoli, I was so upset when I heard you cry out that I couldn't think straight. I needed to get away. Biting his chin seemed like the only way he was going to let me go."

"I saw him throw you down. Are you hurt?"

"No, I don't think so. I am still feeling my heart race with anger. I feel nothing else."

I licked Chica's face. She was my brave friend. "Oh, Chica, didn't those men know we cannot be separated?" We started to walk again with me in the lead and Chica close behind.

As we were getting ready to turn up the street to Maria's shop, I caught wind of a familiar smell. It was the old man. Was he here somewhere? I barked to Chica, and she followed behind me as we bypassed our turn and walked toward the familiar scent.

The scent was coming from the next street, where we saw groups of people. They were gathered in a big yard with many rocks. Some of them were crying. We looked awful, and I didn't want to draw attention to us, so we moved toward the rear of the walled-in yard. I wanted to see if the old man was there. His scent was very strong.

Through an opening in the wall in back, we could see everyone gathered around a long brown box, listening to a man speak to them. The scent of the old man grew stronger. He was there somewhere.

We sat and watched. As soon as the man holding a book was done speaking, people took turns placing flowers on the box. Two men who were standing behind the crowd came forward and lowered the box into the ground. I had a strange feeling the old man was in that box. Many of the people took turns shoveling dirt into the hole. After they were done, the two men who lowered the box now finished shoveling the dirt in the hole until they formed a slight mound of dirt over the box. The people all left as a group, walking to the street.

At one point, I thought I saw Maria, but that person was crying so hard that I wasn't sure. She was holding onto two older women who were also crying. I knew the tears were for the box that was now in the ground. Chica and I watched from our spot, waiting until everyone left.

"Let's go over to the dirt mound," I told her. "I have a feeling that's where the old man is right now." Chica did as I asked.

As we got closer, his scent became stronger. "I think the old man is in the box," I said.

Chica looked up at me and understood. She stepped onto the dirt over the box, lay down, and placed her head on her paws. I did the same. We both began to whimper. The old man was the best thing that had ever happened to us, and now he was gone. Chica and I were lost in our tears with no thoughts of anything else. We couldn't move and didn't want to move.

I could hear a man's voice yelling, "I'll run back and pay the caretaker. I'll be right back." The man went racing up to the little house on the side of this huge yard. His voice was joined by that of another man, who was inside. I could hear them talking. Our great sadness kept us from moving. We were not going anywhere. There was nowhere to go.

The man came out of the little house waving to the man inside. Suddenly, he noticed Chica and me.

"What do you two want? Get off my father's grave! Get out of here!" the man yelled and began to pick up dirt clods and throw them at us. We didn't move. I bared my teeth and began to growl at this man who called the old man his father.

"What's the matter, José Luis? I can hear you yelling from the street." I heard Maria's voice. Chica's head lifted off the dirt. She began to bark and move in circles. "Stop, José Luis! I think those are Papá's two dogs. Perra Pequeña? Perra Grande? Are you under all that dirt and brush? You two look a sight!"

Chica and I both were barking and ran to Maria while José Luis watched us. Chica jumped up on Maria's leg as she had always done when Maria came to visit. I sat by her feet. She bent over and patted us both on our heads.

"You two are the dirtiest perras I have ever seen. I wondered what happened to you when I went to Papá's casa. I called for you and looked everywhere. Papá loved you both so much. I am so happy you found him." She stood up and looked over at the man she called José Luis. Then she turned back to us. "Papá is gone. He left us for a more beautiful place to be with our mother." Maria's eyes teared up, and her voice lowered.

José Luis dropped the dirt clods he was holding onto the ground. He approached us cautiously, and then he knelt and extended his hand.

"Perra Grande, Perra Pequeña, this is José Luis, Papá's only son. I am sure Papá told you about him. I think they look alike. What do you think?" Maria smiled. Then she turned to her brother. "José Luis, please tell Manuel to take Anna and Felix to the house. We have people waiting for the reception. Fortunately, our two aunties can greet our guests until we get there. I need a minute to think what we're going to do with these two beautiful perras." Squatted down, she held my face in one of her hands and Chica's face in her other hand while she spoke.

José Luis ran through the front opening to a waiting car, where he talked to someone in the driver's seat. The man nodded and drove off with Anna and Felix in the back. The kids waved goodbye out the back window as José Luis returned.

"Can you believe this?" Maria asked her brother. "Papá's two dogs show up on the day of his burial. My mind is racing in circles. I know Papá loved these two, but they can't go anywhere with us right now looking like this. We need to get them cleaned and fed. We can decide tomorrow what to do next. Let me think."

All was quiet for a moment while Maria bowed her head in thought. "I've got it! My friend Luz has a small business where she'll wash the dogs, feed them, and board them overnight. She's only down the street." Turning to us, she said, "Come on, perras. We're going for a ride."

We followed Maria to the old man's truck. It was parked close to the entrance to the grounds. We stood by the cab, ready to jump in as we had done many times before. "Oh no, you don't! Papá spoiled you. You two need to jump in the back like other dogs," Maria insisted.

Chica and I stayed close to Maria and followed her to the back of the old man's truck. She opened the tailgate and clapped for us to jump in. We did. She shut the gate. José Luis jumped into the driver's seat while Maria sat in front as his passenger.

We drove a short distance from where we left the old man. When we arrived outside a small white house, we waited for Maria. After she opened the tailgate, we hopped out and walked with her and José Luis to the front door of the casa. The tall woman Maria called Luz opened the screen door and greeted us, and invited us in. She then hugged Maria. "Maria, I am so sorry for your loss. Your Papá always had a wave and a hello when he saw me."

"Thank you, Luz. I miss him terribly, but I know he is finally with my Mamá in heaven. By the way, this is my brother, José Luis. He just flew in from Mexico City." José Luis extended his hand, but Luz ignored it and gave him a hug. "Mucho gusto, José Luis." Then she turned to Maria. "Now, how can I help you?"

Maria explained what she needed as she pointed to us, and Señora Luz nodded. Maria turned to us. "Okay, Perra Grande and Perra Pequeña. You will be cleaned and fed here. I will be back to pick you both up tomorrow."

Señora Luz handed Maria two leashes and two collars. Maria bent down and spoke directly to me. "I am going to put these collars and leashes on you both so Señora Luz can bathe you," she said softly and calmly.

Chica and I both sat perfectly still as Maria attached the collars to our necks and then the leashes to the collars. "You two behave tonight. I will see you mañana." Maria placed her hand on my head and kissed the top of her hand. She did the same for Chica.

Our leashes were handed to Señora Luz. We followed her inside the house and watched from the screen door as the old man's children drove off in his truck. As soon as they were gone, we followed the tall woman through the house to the backyard. Once there, we saw a big pit. She attached our leashes to two hooks on each side of the pit. She didn't need to do that. We weren't going to run. We stood perfectly still as the water sprayed over our heads and bodies. Fortunately for Chica, who was very nervous, Señora Luz washed us together.

It took a while for Señora Luz to soap us down. I looked at the water that came off my soapy body. There was so much dirt. It took a while before the water was no longer brown. I felt the desert and all that we had encountered on our journey wash down the drain. I shook off as much water as I could in the pit while the Señora moved to Chica.

Chica was standing there soapy, waiting her turn. I could see the muddied water sliding off Chica's back, but the Señora was having more difficulty with Chica's hair than mine. There were sticks and pieces of cactus caught in her fluffy white fur. It appeared that the Señora could not get everything off, but she rinsed Chica anyway.

The Señora then moved us to a small patio where we stood perfectly still while she dried us first with a towel and then with a handheld device that blew warm air.

Chica looked like a ball of white. I realized Señora Luz was not finished with Chica yet. From a box, she pulled a small black thing with teeth and plugged it into the wall. When she turned it on, it made a humming sound. Chica was nervous but stayed in place as Señora Luz proceeded to cut her fur. When she was finished, Chica was no longer a ball. She was skinny and so tiny. Chica looked beautiful. I imagined I looked beautiful too.

Señora Luz took us inside to her kitchen, bent down, and took off our leashes, hanging them next to her stove. Then she walked to the cabinet and lifted out a giant bag. It didn't take long for me to realize she was getting us food. We watched as Señora Luz began scooping up familiar pellets and dropping them into the bowls on the counter. "I have a feeling you two know this food. I wonder what you ate while you were living in the desert. If you could only talk, I would have a thousand questions for you."

We could not contain ourselves and started to rush her. "Whoa, perras, sit! Sit down now!" She lightly scolded us, and again, we sat and waited for our bowls to be full. Real food! No more lagartos.

Señora Luz placed the bowls on the floor, saying, "Okay, you can eat now."

Chica and I rushed to the food and ate like we had never eaten before. It was so crunchy and so delicious. After we drank the cold water provided, and relieved ourselves outside, Señora Luz took us to a special bed in a room off the kitchen. I could smell the scent of other dogs who had been there before us.

"Jump up, ladies. You get to sleep in a real bed tonight."

Chica and I jumped up and lay down together. Señora Luz was a nice lady, and she knew we were exhausted. She was smiling as the door closed behind her.

Chica fell fast asleep. It was the first night in a long time that I was not afraid to close my eyes. I was full, clean, and ready to take on whatever lay ahead of us. I thought about the old man and how happy I was that Maria had found him, and how happy Maria seemed to be to have found us. It was all good. It was all …

Chapter 16

AND THEY LIVED HAPPILY …

When I heard a door open, I pulled myself out of a deep sleep. I sat up, taking a minute to think about how I got here. Chica felt me move, and she, too, sat up, facing the door.

"Are you two ready for breakfast and a chance to get outside? Come on. Let's go outside first."

We followed Señora Luz out the door to the yard in the back. It was large with a high fence around it. We were the only perras there. Chica and I ran to a bush and a rock that we both found perfect for our needs and squatted next to both. Afterward, we started running around the yard. It felt good knowing we were safe. Señora Luz called us to come as she held the door open.

As we entered the kitchen, I could see our bowls were filled with lots of pellets of familiar dog food. There was another large bowl on the side, filled with water. Señora Luz was a very nice lady who smiled while she watched us eat.

Fully satisfied, I looked around and spotted blankets on the floor next to the stove. I knew the blankets were for perras just like me to rest on. After I got comfortable, Chica walked over and joined me. We both watched from our shared blanket as Señora Luz went about her cooking.

The familiar sounds of pots clanging together and the smells of food simmering on the stove brought memories of the old man. He was the kindest person I had ever known, and except for my Mamá and Chica, I had never felt love like I did from him. We were his best friends. Almost daily, he would talk to us, teach us words, and even sing to us. Unfortunately, he wasn't that good of a singer, but he would laugh after each song, take off his hat, and bow. We would bark in appreciation. He loved us and we loved him.

I felt so comfortable and at home in Señora Luz's kitchen. As I was enjoying the familiar smells and sounds of the kitchen, a thought popped into my head: *What will happen to Chica and me?* We had been sisters for so long, I could not imagine life without her. I felt a tear when the realization hit me: *No one wants to give two dogs a home. We'll be lucky if they even want one of us. Who am I kidding? Of course, everyone is going to want Chica. She's so cute and hardly eats anything; besides, she'll gladly dance on her hind legs for supper.*

Then there's me. No one will want a big dog that eats a lot. I'm not pretty like Chica, or cuddly. I'm a good hunter, but who needs a hunter in this town? I couldn't even think about it anymore. It made me very sad. As the old man would often say, "Things have a way of working out." Maybe that was what I needed to think about.

"Perra Grande and Perra Pequeña, I think I hear a truck coming for you. They will be so surprised when they see you." Señora Luz smiled as she spoke excitedly.

Chica and I jumped up and followed her to the door. Through the screen, we saw the familiar red truck parked in the driveway. Maria opened her door first and got out of the truck. José Luis did the same, closing his door behind him. Señora Luz opened the screen to welcome them. Chica and I both instinctively ran to Maria.

Maria reached out and petted each of us. I sat down next to her, and Chica, as always, jumped on her leg. "Perra Pequeña, get down.

Why can't you be more like Perra Grande? Papá spoiled you just because you're so cute."

Looking up at Señora Luz, Maria spoke. "I really don't recognize these two dogs. I don't remember them ever looking this good. Thank you, Luz."

"And you will not believe how much they ate. Fortunately, they were so tired that I had no problem getting them to sleep. I can't even imagine what they encountered while in the desert. If only these perras could talk." Maria and José Luis stood there thinking about what Señora Luz had just said.

José Luis walked over and thanked Señora Luz while pulling out some pesos. "I included the two collars on the bill," Señora Luz told him. She smiled and presented him with a piece of paper. He smiled back and gave her the money. Then he looked at Maria, and they started toward the truck.

He called out to Chica and me. "Let's go, ladies. It's time to head home. We have a lot to do."

Head home? I was not sure what that meant, but we climbed into the back of the truck and sat proudly as José Luis shut the tailgate. Maria and José Luis sat in the front. It felt nice to be in the old man's truck again. It felt nice to be clean and fed.

After goodbyes were exchanged with the Señora, we headed down the road. The smells coming from the homes were familiar. As we drove down the street, I felt a little nervous not knowing what was in store for us, but I trusted Maria. She was family.

Without warning, I smelled that familiar smell of the old man. I'm not sure what came over me. I found myself jumping from the moving truck and running to that hump of dirt I knew to be him.

José Luis must have seen me jump to the street through his rear-view mirror because he immediately pulled over to the side of the road. Chica unsuccessfully tried to jump out, prompting José Luis to open the tailgate so she could. She ran and threw herself next to me. We both lay on the old man's spot while Maria and José Luis walked over to us.

Maria leaned on her brother's shoulder and held his arm. Tears started to form in her eyes. I could hear her speaking to her brother. "José, look how they lie there. They really loved Papá. I miss him so much. I can only imagine how much they miss him."

José smiled and patted his sister's arm. They walked over to us. Maria placed her hand on the dirt. José Luis put his hands on our backs and spoke softly. "We know how much you loved Papá and how you must be missing him. I wish things could have been different. I regret not taking time to spend with him. I let my work come first. Thank God he had you two and most of all Maria." José bowed his head.

"José Luis, Maria, is that you?" a voice said, coming from the street. An elderly woman with dark gray hair made into a braid and wrapped around the top of her head was heading toward us with flowers in her arms.

"Señora Vasquez, so nice to see you." Maria approached her with her arms open. Hugs and kisses ensued from both José Luis and Maria.

"I wanted to pay my respects since I did not make it to the funeral. I brought a few flowers from my garden to place on your father's grave. I'm guessing where his dogs are sitting is where he is buried. How many times did I see your Papá with those two perras, and now he's in heaven with your Mamá."

Señora Vasquez stepped closer and placed the flowers on the grave, bowed, and pulled her shawl tighter around her shoulders. José Luis reached out to hold her arm. He continued holding it as she stepped away from the old man's grave.

Maria smiled and hugged her again. Then Señora Vasquez turned to José Luis and asked, "Will you be here for a while, José?"

"I am planning to relocate to my father's farm," José Luis said. "It will be a perfect place to paint, and Maria knows some galleries in town that she's sure will display my work. I will be doing what I was doing in Mexico City except I'll be home, with my sister and her family, and my four-legged friends."

Both ladies smiled when he said those words and looked at Chica and me.

"I have a home, a job, and two perras to protect me here. I know my Papá would approve."

I began barking at Chica. "He wants us to live with him at the old man's casa! We will be okay, Chica! The old man saved us once from death; now through his son, he has saved us once again."

As I looked to the sky, my thoughts were directed to the old man. *Your son has returned. Your prayers have been answered.*

Señora Vasquez smiled her approval at what José had said and kissed Maria and José goodbye. Then she turned and walked away.

Chica and I followed José Luis and Maria back to the truck. I felt sadness leaving my body, and taking its place, hope. We had a home again, and we were needed.

Chica and I jumped into the back of the truck. Then José Luis got behind the wheel and turned on the engine. Chica stood close to me, while I stretched and sat down. "Chica, we are going home. José Luis will take care of us, and we will take care of him. How do you feel about that?"

Chica wagged her tail and started barking. I joined in. Maria turned her head and looked through the back window. She saw two very happy dogs barking in the back of the truck. Everything was going to be okay. We had lost the old man, but Maria had gained a brother, and we found a family again.

I wondered if Maria could see me smiling. I was driving home with the old man's son at the wheel and my best friend at my side. Chica and I were beginning a new story. Then out of nowhere, the old man's words popped into my head once again: "Have faith. Things have a way of working out." He was right!

Printed in the United States
by Baker & Taylor Publisher Services